# MY HUSBAND

# My Husband

## THE EXTRAORDINARY HISTORY OF
## NICHOLAS BROME

ANNE ELLIOTT

Matador
9 Priory Business Park,
Wistow Road, Kibworth Beauchamp,
Leicestershire. LE8 0RX
Tel: 0116 279 2299
Email: books@troubador.co.uk
Web: www.troubador.co.uk/matador
Twitter: @matadorbooks


ISBN 978 1789013 122

British Library Cataloguing in Publication Data.
A catalogue record for this book is available from the British Library.

Printed and bound in Great Britain by 4Edge Limited
Typeset in 11pt Adobe Garamond Pro by Troubador Publishing Ltd, Leicester, UK

Matador is an imprint of Troubador Publishing Ltd

For my family and friends
on both sides of the Atlantic

Our pleasure here is all vain glory
This false world is but transitory
The flesh is brittle, the Fiend is sly:
The fear of death disturbs me

'*Timor Mortis Conturbat Me*'
William Dunbar, Late C15th

I

As I open the heavy oak door and step down into the church of St. James at Baddesley Clinton, I tread on the head of Nicholas Brome. I know that beneath my feet, after ten full years in the ground, he must be riddled with maggots and worms, his flesh rotted completely away. Yet surely his bones still stand where he was buried, much to the horror and reluctance of the gravediggers, upright, wakeful.

Despite the time that has passed since his body was lowered with difficulty into its deep vertical tomb, the image of him standing in the earth is still so vivid that when it catches me unawares I am overwhelmed with grief. Then I try to comfort myself with the thought that someday his dear bones too will decay and he will at last become dust. Perhaps then, against his will, he might finally find rest, he who was once so high, lord of this manor, the King's Sheriff for Warwickshire – and my husband.

I close the door against the bright spring sunshine, the profusion of bluebells, the fresh green leaves, and turn into the cool stillness of the church. There is no way to avoid standing on the brass portrait of Nicholas in his fine armor. It covers the slab of marble above his grave, immediately inside the doorway, walked over by all who enter. Everything is just as he intended. The inscription below the portrait is simple and its plea heartfelt: 'Nicholas Brome died on the tenth day of October in the year of our Lord one thousand five hundred and sixteen. Pray for his soul.'

1

Moving quickly aside, I drop to my knees. I ask God, Our Lady Mary, St. Catherine, and all the angels to forgive Nicholas his terrible sins, to remember always his good works, which must surely outweigh the bad, and to find a place for him with them in Heaven. It is a prayer I have offered up humbly every day since he left us, a prayer I shall utter with my own dying breath and a prayer that I all but know in my heart is futile.

Remembering my present purpose, I rise and turn excitedly towards the dark wooden altar where I see at once the object of my visit: above the altar with sunlight streaming through its panes in a myriad of colours is an amazing new window. Motes of dust hang in the beams of red and blue, and it is more wonderful than anything I could possibly have dreamed of. Earlier this afternoon, as I left my children at the manor house to spend time with their cousins and hurried here eagerly along the path between the oaks, I remembered Constance's explanation of the detailed plans that she and Edward had drawn up for an East window that would adequately commemorate her father and reflect the piety of their family. I knew that she wanted something splendid to compensate for the obscure manner of Nicholas's burial, which she found profoundly unsatisfactory. I knew that Edward would spare no expense to honour his father-in-law. But this, this is something beyond my imagination.

High above me, in the central panel of the window with light flowing all around him, our Lord hangs upon his cross, his head drooping dolefully beneath a wreath of vivid green and a halo of azure blue, his face full of suffering. I fall to my knees in awe, 'Lord, forgive us our sins'. Saints stand in panels on either side of our Lord, their heads haloed by white light fringed with yellow: St. George spearing the dragon, his short cloak and the cross on his breast a dazzling red; and St. Catherine, I smile with delight to see her, my favourite saint, grasping her sword and wheel, elegant in purest purple and gold. At the base of the cross stand St. John

2

and St. Mary Magdalene, and there in a panel just to their left, at the heart of the holy scene, kneels Nicholas.

He looks just as I remember him, just as he looked on the day he took me, Lettice Catesby, to be his third wife: a man approaching seventy yet still vigorous, with thick white hair and beard. His armour gleams beneath a black surcoat embroidered in red, gold and white and emblazoned on the sleeve with his emblem, three sprigs of broom. He kneels on a rich purple cushion with golden tassels. The ornate tiled floor is much like the one here in the church of St. James and the intricately decorated columns framing the scene are also familiar. The detail is astonishing. I go closer to look into my husband's face. The artist has captured his likeness so well. I peer into the brightness and am almost sure I see a fearful anxiety in his eyes as he prays there among the saints, an open bible before him.

The window is truly a remarkable thing. Constance has planned it with such care. She and Edward are there, kneeling together in the panel corresponding to her father's, to the right of the foot of the cross. They too are in splendid array made all the more dazzling by the sunshine. I am delighted to see how their piety shines through the glass. They are such a devout couple. If anyone's prayers can save Nicholas's soul, it will be theirs. They appear again in the upper panels of the window, Constance kneeling with their five daughters and Edward with their three sons. I am glad that they named their youngest son after Nicholas, and it is lovely too to know that Constance is soon to have another child, her ninth. He has so many descendants.

The effect of the imagery is, as Constance intended, to show Nicholas as the man of status he was, a man of wealth, culture and prayer, a man at the heart of a great family. This is the father she loved and the man I married. And the window does not overstate his worth; there is more to him even than this. I think of his other children – Elizabeth and Edward, such fine young people, who were born to his second wife, Katherine, and who I love as mine; and our own dear little ones, Ralph, Anne and Joyce, who hardly knew their father and yet are growing strong and healthy. I think of his houses, his lands and tenants, his work for the King and the country. The window captures him forever, a man of such substance. I feel sure that all those who enter this church in all the years to come, and tread upon him and see the window, will be moved to pray for his soul. Such is the power of the window that I wonder if perhaps after all Constance is right: Nicholas will eventually escape the sufferings of purgatory and find a place in Heaven.

Suddenly it is as if the light blows out. A cloud must have passed across the sun and the window loses its vibrant glow. It is just coloured glass after all. I sit on a step below the altar and gather my cloak around me in the gloom of what is now the unlit church. No, I remind myself, Constance's faith in her father's redemption is based on an ignorance of the truth. She believes she knows the extent of his sins; he didn't attempt to hide the crimes of his impetuous youth and often produced the pardons he had received from King Henry VII and the Pope when he wanted to reassure her that his slate had been wiped clean. But if she knew the full horror of his sins as I do, she would not be so confident.

I almost wish now that I had not begged him to share his secret, to confess to me at least, if he would not to a priest. He was close to death; his heart was giving out and there was no more to be done for him. At last he was forced to face the fear of death that he had held at bay for years by living life to the full. I remember all his talk was of Hell: its fire, its agony. Naturally I tried to reassure him. Although I had been his wife for just six years, I had been aware of him all my life and both the rash deeds of his younger days and his quest for forgiveness were well known to me. I reminded him that, as he had repented and made ample amends for his past mistakes, as he had been pardoned by the Pope, who surely is God's representative upon this earth, he did not need to fear Hell. While he might have to endure a period in purgatory, it was certain to be mercifully brief; so many mourners would pray for his soul that he would soon find himself among the righteous in the kingdom of Heaven.

It was then that he told me there was something more, another crime he had committed, a mortal sin for which, he knew with certainty, there could never be forgiveness.

I remember how I urged him to confide in me. Surely he had done nothing so terrible that our Heavenly Father would not find it in His heart to forgive? I was so concerned that Nicholas should be spared the punishments of purgatory that would certainly come to him if he died without confessing his sins. Now, I almost regret that he ever unburdened himself to me, for if he had not, I too might retain some hope of his salvation. Instead I live with a terrible dread that the passage of his soul was not through purgatory at all – but the swift route straight to Hell.

||

S itting on the stone cold step below the altar in the growing gloom of the now late afternoon, I imagine all those who will enter the church in the many days and years to come. As they tread on my husband's grave, will they pray for his soul? As they walk upon his head and picture him standing upright in the ground, will they feel compassion? If I could tell them everything, everything about the way he lived and died, would they find it in their hearts to forgive?

Nicholas was sixty-one when we married and I, a virgin still, was thirty-six. He had already lived a life as full as any man's and survived more blows, some would say, than one man should. By then he was nearing the end of his story and I knew it had been a colourful one, for snippets of it reached our corner of Northamptonshire, enlivening my quiet days. My own life had been mundane, my world small, enclosed as it was by the borders of our Catesby family lands and the limitations that arose from my being a girl. All, including myself, had assumed that I would never marry. My mother died when I was eleven and I had taken it upon myself to fill her shoes, caring for my two brothers, managing the house, looking after my father, and along the way acquiring as much understanding of the wider world as I could; for I had inherited my mother's inquiring mind and her love of knowledge. It was my good fortune that she had persuaded my father to allow me to attend lessons with my brothers whenever my household duties allowed, and so I learned to read and write, both English and a little Latin. I read everything that I could find; I kept a commonplace book where I recorded phrases and verses that appealed to me; and I listened. I listened to my father talking with my brothers and with his household men about what was happening in our county and in the country at large. I listened to the gossip among the servants and to the news brought to us at Newnham by our cousin, George Catesby, who lived at Lapworth in Warwickshire, just three miles across the fields from Baddesley. And when I listened I heard about Nicholas Brome.

He was born into violence. Just hours after he came into the world, while his mother, Beatrice, was still lying-in at the manor house, the thundering of hooves and a hammering on the door announced the arrival of a messenger, both horse and rider drenched in sweat. He was one of the Bromes' household men who had ridden full-pelt from Warwick to warn her that Bromesplace, their ancient family house in the town, had been attacked, its doors broken down.

"They came with force, Madam, and fully armed. Unruly men. At least a dozen, maybe more, with broad swords, pole-axes and arrows, and as I left to bring you word, they were entering the place," he gasped for breath, his eyes wide with alarm as he took in the scene, his mistress abed in her smock and the infant suckling. "I fear that when they find the master is away, they will come on here to Baddesley to search for him."

"But what can I do?" she demanded, drawing up her knees beneath the bedsheet and hugging Nicholas tightly to her. 'With John in London, I am alone".

"You must secure the house, Madam. They will be fast behind me. With your leave, I will stir the servants."

"Yes, yes, please do what you can, only first send my children to me."

She threw on her gown, gathered her little family and retreating from the upper chambers, hurried them to the tower room where, having locked and bolted the heavy oak door from within, they cowered together, the babe in her arms, his older brother Thomas and their sisters clinging to her knees. With growing dread they listened to the preparations being made by the house servants: the rush of men to the gatehouse, the orders to raise the drawbridges protecting the outer and inner moats, the calls of tenants and friends asking for time to cross so they could help defend the hall, the barring of doors. They heard the clamour in the gatehouse as the men arrayed themselves, pulled padded jackets and helmets from coffers, took up their bows, prepared the shot.

Though terrified, Beatrice tried to reassure the children that the hall was secure, that their father had foreseen this moment and made plans. She reminded them that in the floor of the tower room there was a trap door and she showed them the way it opened into the cellar passage. If their defences were breached, she told them, if the ruffians came and succeeded in gaining entry to the hall, they would escape this way. Once through the trap door, they would move carefully along the passage, at first they would be able to stand but as they neared the east end, the ground would slope up and they would have to scramble on their knees. They would find a plank on the floor of the passage and they would all have to work together to slide this out through a niche and across to the far bank of the moat. Crawling over this, she told them, was how they would make their escape.

Angry cries cut the night air as the attackers from Warwick approached. They were a riotous mob, armed and arrayed as if it was a land of war. Two were on horses, fully regaled and bearing the emblem of the bear and ragged staff, while the rest of the rabble were on foot.

They found the manor house quiet and in darkness. On hearing their approach the defending bowmen in the gatehouse, already in position to either side of the great oak door, took aim through the loopholes. The gunmen too remained poised, peering through their sighting slits to pick out individuals in the gloom. The stone farm buildings beside the moat were silent too. Moments passed, as the assailants seemed uncertain what to do. Beatrice cuddled Nicholas close and gestured to the other children to remain silent. Isabella and Elizabeth clung together shaking, while Thomas held two year old Agnes tight, putting his hand across her mouth lest she, too young to realize their predicament, should cry out.

A sudden shout from one of the mob broke the tension. He had sighted a poor, hapless man making his way along the lane towards the town in the first light of dawn. They fell upon him, shrieking savagely and threatening to kill him if he did not tell them all he knew about how many people were in the manor house and what weapons they might have. Learning from his panic-stricken stammering that the place was well armed, the group gathered to confer and this was the moment when the men in the gatehouse let loose their shots and arrows with all the speed and might they could muster. The noise was terrifying. Nicholas began to wail in his mother's arms and the other children screamed and sobbed.

Their terror was well founded. Repelled by the heavy fire from the manor house and thwarted, the frenzied mob fell upon the neighbouring cottage of John Underwood, one of the Brome's tenants, and broke in there instead. Finding Underwood at home, they beat him senseless and left him for dead. His wife, who was great with child and nearly at her time, they spared but she saw it all and was thrown into such a state of fear and sorrow that she was distraught for many days after and never fully regained her wits.

The fate of the Underwoods would have been theirs, Nicholas was sure of it, had not their father had the foresight to ensure that the manor house was well prepared. He never tired of hearing his mother recount the tale, though it made his blood boil. He would ask her to list the names of those who had threatened them: they were all the Earl of Warwick's men and included the town's bailiffs and barkers; craftsmen and yeomen; and even the baker, Thomas

Stone. He seethed at the injustice of it. Once when Beatrice was telling her sons the story, his brother claimed he had pleaded to be allowed to arm himself and join the men defending the hall. But their mother had laughed at the very idea and said, "Thomas, you were as afraid as the girls." Nicholas knew he would not have been afraid. Burning anger rose within him whenever he thought of that night, all his life it was ready to spark.

Yes, I reflect, violence was ever present for my husband, even in his infancy. At Warwick Castle, Richard Neville, the new Earl, was stirring the men of Warwickshire against King Henry VI and those, like John Brome, who supported him. The king seemed powerless to keep the land at peace. The unruly men who threatened Baddesley, men Nicholas knew to be so much less than his father in every way, had come hot from their assault on Bromesplace in Warwick where his family, the Brome family, had lived peacefully since time immemorial. There the mob had destroyed the walls and hedges, broken down the hall door, which had been locked strong and fast, and entered the property. Finding his father absent, they had shattered the glass windows, smashed through the doors and forced open the coffers. Having rifled through the contents of chambers and chests, they stole away goods to the value of 100 marks, a huge sum, as well as money and quantities of legal papers, many of which belonged to the Brome family but others that were being stored by John, a lawyer, for safe keeping on behalf of his clients. The events of that night had caused his father great and unbearable hurt and the full implications of the loss would never be known. Later John hid the threat he had felt by joking to Nicholas that the worst of it was that the mob had drunk, carried off or poured away all the wine in his cellar. He did not speak of what might have been if they had found him at home that night.

As Deputy Chamberlain and Under-treasurer to the Exchequer, John Brome had been in London on royal business on the night when his second son was born and his properties in Warwickshire were attacked. It was July 1450. He hurried home full of outrage and bringing news of even more shocking violence in the capital. Years later he told his sons that he had seen with his own eyes, outside the Tower, the severed heads of many of the King's household men, put on pikes and made to kiss each other. One of the heads had been the Lord High Treasurer himself, John's own master. The sight had shocked and sickened him to his heart. It was the work of rebels from Kent, who had swarmed across London Bridge led by one Jack Cade. Some said they numbered five thousand men and included not only peasants, craftsmen and shopkeepers, but soldiers and sailors returning from the French wars, and even, it was rumoured, some knights and squires: all united in opposition to the King's rule. It was without doubt a time of great rebellion throughout the land.

"Where were the King and Queen when all this was happening?" my husband had asked his father incredulously, wondering why they had not responded with equal force.

"Mercifully, upon hearing word of the mob gathering on Blackheath, they had removed themselves to the castle at Kenilworth. But it was shocking to realize that on the very night that the rioters came to our hall doors here at Baddesley, the King, our sovereign lord, was not more than five miles away. They behaved in that unlawful way with no fear or dread of him."

John told his sons that the rebel, Cade, having proclaimed himself Lord Mayor and made such a hideous example of the King's closest men, had gone on to lead his followers in looting the city. Only a battle on London Bridge itself, with many casualties on both sides, had at last caused his forces to retreat.

"When finally the traitor, John Cade, was killed, his body was dragged into the City. I was there myself and saw it quartered, and his head put upon a pike on London Bridge along with the heads of many who had supported him."

Their father's tales of the horrors he had seen always shocked his sons but they begged to hear them time and again.

In the face of the turbulence and uncertainty around him Nicholas grew strong and healthy. I put this down to his mother's care and her determination to remain quietly at Baddesley and keep Nicholas with her. Beatrice loved the manor house that she and John had built together and far preferred to spend her time there than at Bromesplace or their London house. She disliked the bustle of Warwick, particularly now it owed its allegiance to Richard Neville, and city life held no attraction for her. As long as she was able to obtain the goods she needed by sending servants or asking John to make purchases for her, she was delighted to stay in the manor house where she could enjoy the peace of her gardens and fishpools.

She could not retreat completely from the world, of course. As John was in the service of the King and was anxious to maintain his interests in the City, he spent much of his time in London and he and his household men brought her regular news. She heard that even there, Richard Neville was making his presence felt. In her view, he did not deserve the earldom that he had gained only by virtue of being married to the old Earl of Warwick's daughter. He was a schemer and could not be trusted to use his new power well. If only the old Earl, Richard Beauchamp, had had a healthy brood of boys, this upstart Neville would be of no consequence in their lives, but it was not so.

Nicholas's family owed their allegiance and much of their success to Beauchamp. As a young boy, John Brome had been placed in the household of the old Earl at Warwick Castle. His parents, living at Bromesplace in the shadow of the castle and seeing that their son was exceptionally quick witted and eager to learn, had brought him to the Earl's attention.

It was in Beauchamp's household that John learned to read and write in both Latin and French, to understand the elements of religion and the basis of the law. Beauchamp was guardian of the young King Henry VI and had sole charge of his instruction. Occasionally he would bring the King to Warwick Castle and John and the other boys of the household would join him in his lessons. Many held Beauchamp to be the finest thinker of the age and John would hang on his every word as he related noble tales of his military exploits against the French and the adventures that had befallen him on his pilgrimage to the Holy Land. John's education included all the social accomplishments expected of a gentleman: good manners and self-discipline, dancing, singing, and all the courtly skills. Physical pursuits, though they had to be mastered, held less of an attraction for him. In this my husband, always so full of vigour, so delighting in physical activity, differed greatly from his father. Certainly John learned to ride, to hunt and to hawk, to fight with dagger and sword, as was expected, but his interest and passion was always for learning and the law. Beauchamp picked him out at an early age as having a sharp mind and saw to it that he was sent to Clifford's Inn in London to continue his legal training.

Nicholas always spoke to me so proudly of his father, of the time John spent in the service of such a noble lord as Richard Beauchamp and of the way he had built himself up from nothing to be a lawyer, a landowner and a gentleman of substance. For John had thrown himself into his studies, becoming shrewd and adept at drafting writs and pleading in the courts, and soon entered royal service in the Court of the Exchequer. As his wealth grew, he used his legal knowledge to help him acquire lands and properties, including Baddesley and, some six miles distant, the manor of Woodloes, which is now my home.

Nicholas was born at the height of his father's success: just the previous year John had been confirmed in his position as Deputy Chamberlain and Under-treasurer at the Exchequer for life by the King himself. There had been much rejoicing at Baddesley but neither John nor Beatrice had dared to believe that the family's future was now secure. The attacks on their property confirmed their sense of unease.

Beatrice kept her children close and I'm sure that as she nursed Nicholas, she took comfort in the knowledge that the manor house's defences had proved strong and true. But they were strange, uncertain times when Fortune's wheel turned fast and their happiness rose and fell with it. In August, John received a further honour from the King. He sent a messenger to Baddesley with the news that he had been appointed to act as Under-sheriff of Worcestershire. Beatrice wrote to her husband at once of her delight and pride, but that very same evening some of their other properties in Warwickshire came under attack and she was forced to send word next day of the costly repairs to hedges and fences that would be necessary.

Towards the end of the year as she made plans for Christmas, when John would return from London for a week of feasting and merrymaking, Beatrice received a letter from him that gave substance to all their unease about Neville.

*'Trusty and well beloved wife, I write with heavy heart to tell you that our fears about the motives of my lord of Warwick have proved wholly justified, for today the 7th day of December, early in the morning, he came to the place where I was in Westminster Hall and forcibly demanded of me the keys to the coffers of the Exchequer. I had little option but to hand them over to him for upon my enquiring to know on whose authority he came, he produced a royal patent of recognition granting him the Chamberlainship. Wife, I can only think that to come by such a patent he has pressured the King with great threats, and that in this he had the support of my lord, the Duke of York, who is lately returned from Ireland. The result is that I have been ejected from my office and my lord of Warwick is free to appoint his own man. There being nothing further to keep me here*

*at present I will ride for Baddesley tomorrow and will be with you by Sunday, God willing.'*

Beatrice kept the letter and years later showed it to Nicholas. He knew it marked a pivotal moment for his father. Although John was later restored to his position at the Exchequer, he now understood that he could no longer rely on the high regard of the King to keep him in office. He saw that the new Earl of Warwick was a man who dared to question the power of God's anointed King and who would go to great lengths to further his own interests.

I remember Nicholas telling me how proud he was that his father remained staunchly loyal to King Henry and the house of Lancaster even when he knew that this was likely to bring him into conflict with others in Warwickshire who would set their store by Neville. My husband knew that to remain true to what is right even in the face of danger demands great courage. His father might not have been a fighting man but his bravery certainly could not be denied.

|||

I t comforts me now to know that my husband enjoyed much happiness in his youth. While the threats to John's properties and position were ever present, Nicholas thrived in the clear, country air of Baddesley where he spent his infancy. Beatrice was determined to keep Nicholas at home with her for as long as she could. Despite their disputes with Warwick, John had insisted that their first-born son, Thomas, should be placed in the Earl's household from the age of six, just as he himself had been. Beatrice knew he shared her misgivings about Warwick's growing support for the Duke of York and her fears that Thomas might be influenced to favour York above the King. But John remained convinced that growing up at Warwick Castle with the sons of nobles and gentlemen would give Thomas the best possible training for life.

It seemed to Beatrice that the dank air of Warwick Castle made Thomas sickly. So she allowed Nicholas to run free, with only the warning that he should not go near the quarry at Badger's Dell, and he occupied his days with venturing out into the fields to help feed the cattle, roaming in Hay Wood, exploring the contents of the fishpools and chasing rabbits in the warrens. As he grew older, he learned to ride and to hunt. When his younger brother John, was old enough to join him, the two boys would frequently take bread and cheese from the kitchens wrapped in muslin cloths and spend the day fishing in the Great Pond or wandering the lanes towards Woodloes Manor where their father had recently acquired new meadows and grazing lands.

The time came, of course, when he had to begin his education. Beatrice and his older sisters had taught him to read and write and pay attention to his prayers but for Latin and French he needed more formal instruction. Beatrice remained set against his joining the service of any noble lord; it was so hard to be sure where anyone's allegiance lay. York's power in the country was growing and even many of their friends who had been consistently loyal to King Henry were wavering. So the decision was made that Nicholas should attend the grammar school in Warwick before beginning legal training and joining his father's Inn in London.

Unlike his mother, Nicholas loved the town of Warwick with its churches and fine houses. The grammar school was held in the Church of St. John the Baptist that stood in the market square at the heart of the bustling streets. He enjoyed the variety of living at Bromesplace on the days when he attended school and returning to Baddesley to hunt and fish and spend time with his mother whenever he was free of lessons.

Bromesplace stood on the south bank of the River Avon at the foot of the town's bridge. Warwick Castle rose imposingly above it to the north. It was a sprawling house, extended and improved by generations of his father's family. Its dark hall housed coffers and treasure boxes. Nicholas imagined the coffers were filled with documents and deeds relating to John Brome's legal practice and was in awe of his father's learning. He knew how important it was that his father had an understanding of the law sharp enough to defend their property against rival claims. The name Herthill was familiar to him from a young age and that of Catesby too. For, yes, my own family of Catesby was in dispute with John Brome for many years over properties in Lapworth, and we respected him as a shrewd and formidable adversary. Nicholas knew his father had been meticulous in ascertaining the ownership of all the lands and properties he purchased. As John Brome had become rich through his work for King Henry and the royal household, he had built up his estates to match his newfound status and Nicholas was immensely proud of him.

Beatrice felt that Bromesplace belonged very much to the Bromes and she had never really taken to it, preferring the home she and John had built together at Baddesley. As a consequence it was never much used by the family. This suited Nicholas who was happy to find his own sleeping space in one of the several small chambers that opened off the hall and then to spend as much time of his free time as possible in vigorous outdoor pursuits.

My husband was not a studious boy. He had his father's quick mind but he disliked repetitive tasks and once he had done enough to satisfy his tutors, he would be off riding the lanes towards Barford and Stratford or exploring the town of Warwick on foot. He particularly delighted in watching the final stages in the construction of the Beauchamp Chapel at St. Mary's Church. It was being built to honour his father's old master, Richard Beauchamp, a man who Nicholas knew as the epitome of courtly virtues, and the splendor of the place was a testament to Beauchamp's nobility.

Soon after we married, Nicholas suggested that we visit Warwick together so he could show me Beauchamp's wonderful chapel. I had only ever passed through the town before and it was his particular pleasure to show me the place that meant so much to him. We chose the day of the feast of St. George to walk the two miles from our home at Woodloes. There was to be a fair and Nicholas knew the town would be looking its best, with banners of the red cross hanging along the streets and the whole place bustling with traders and entertainers. There was also a chance that, if the crowds of pilgrims could be passed through, in addition to seeing the chapel, we might catch a glimpse of the church of St. Mary's most holy treasures, displayed only upon this St. George's day: a horn of glory that had once belonged to the saint himself, a fragment of his most venerable knee and a stone upon which a drop of his blood fell as he was martyred for his worship of our Lord.

It was early afternoon and, although the mass was over, we heard the bells of St. Mary's peeling long before we entered the North Gate. The street was thronged with merry makers, many wearing a red rose upon their sleeve or cap, and several called out, 'God bless England' or 'God bless St. George' as we passed. It seemed that a thousand candles must have been lit within St. Mary's, as its windows glowed warmly, drawing us forward.

I took my husband's arm. We had dressed richly for the occasion and I thought how well my small hand looked with its heavy ruby ring against the purple velvet of his wide sleeve, slashed as it was in the latest way to reveal a silver-grey satin beneath. I was aware that my blue damask gown was fetching too, fitting tightly over my slim waist and hips, falling to the ground in flowing folds and embroidered with more silver stars than filled the heavens. We made an elegant couple and I smiled at the wonder of it.

"Nicholas, thank you for bringing me to Warwick on such a joyous afternoon. It is truly as delightful a place as you described."

He turned to me with his easy smile. "I could not let you reach the age of forty without seeing St. George's knee, now could I? Let's see if we can clear a route through this crowd and get inside."

I remember feeling the comfort of his body as he put his arm protectively around my shoulders and held me close, guiding me through the throng towards the open doors of the church. It was something I had not been prepared for – his warmth, his physical tenderness. I had not expected to know the physical affection that can be between man and wife. As a young woman I had remained at home with my father, caring for him and managing the household. Now I had a husband past his sixtieth year, older even than Father. The ease and pleasure of his touch had taken me completely by surprise.

We never did see the piece of bone held in a jewel encrusted casket, nor yet the vial containing a drop of our Lady Mary's blood that the pilgrims pressed to glimpse, but Beauchamp's chantry chapel was truly wondrous to behold, just as Nicholas had promised it would be. The Earl was buried in a magnificent marble tomb that stood in the centre of the chapel and upon it lay his gilded effigy. Nicholas and I stood long, looking at the amazing detail of his armour and his careworn hands, held slightly apart, through which he appeared to gaze Heavenwards. Following his eyes upwards we saw high above the painted figure of our Lady, Queen of Heaven, who seemed to smile down upon us. Around us were many beautiful windows, allowing light to fill the chapel even late on an April afternoon, windows full of angels: angels singing, angels playing instruments, angels creating music to carry Beauchamp's soul on its journey.

And there were saints too, delicately carved: St. Barbara, St. Mary Magdalene, St Margaret, and, my own favourite, the blessed St. Catherine, reading from the bible. With God in his Majesty at the moment of the Last Judgement looking down on us from high on the west wall, the paint still fresh, the colours vivid, and priests in the choir intoning their prayers for Beauchamp's soul, I felt that we too had entered the kingdom of Heaven.

I turned to Nicholas, sensing that he was also moved by the painting, and glimpsed the foreboding in his face before he shook it off and replaced it with a smile. It saddened me to know that despite repenting of his sins and atoning for the crimes of his youth in so many ways, he still feared death.

"Shall we pray, husband?" I asked, and we crossed the chapel to kneel at the steps before the altar, where we remained for some minutes in silent contemplation.

Before we left the chapel I asked Nicholas about the gilded figures who stood around the base of Beauchamp's tomb, each different and surely modeled from life. Did he know who they were?

"They are Beauchamp's weepers," he explained. "Relatives of his, friends and fellow lords who mourn his passing. One I know to be Richard Neville, whose treachery was yet unknown at the time the tomb was planned."

I regretted my question at once, knowing the deep hurt that Warwick had caused his family. I was sorry to provoke memories that caused him pain.

He took my arm and led me away saying, "But let's not spoil the afternoon with thoughts of the man. Let's walk in the Dean's garden. We might find peace there even on such a busy afternoon. Or shall we take a look at the stalls in the market place? I should love to buy you a pretty trinket as a reminder of this St. George's day."

So we left the chapel and made our way to the south porch of the church where Nicholas brightened as he showed me the steps that led up to the library over the door where he had sometimes taken his lessons as a boy. He recalled the desperate tedium of copying passages from the manuscripts held there and how he would long to be outside practicing archery or fighting with sword and dagger. Even dancing would have been a joy.

As a child, Nicholas saw very little of his elder brother, Thomas, and I would imagine that the boys were as chalk and cheese. Beatrice was probably right to think that the atmosphere at Warwick Castle was responsible for making her first born weak, not just in his health, which was always frail, but in his spirit too. For at the castle, Thomas came under the influence of men whose desire for power took precedence over all. Warwick gathered around him men who were keen to advance their prospects, through the use of force if necessary. She and John watched with growing unease as Warwick threw his support behind the Duke of York in opposition to the King.

The Bromes were ardent Lancastrians, as were my own family, and it was a great blow to them all when, during the Spring of

1461, in the thirty-eight year of his reign, King Henry was forced to flee to Scotland and the Duke of York's son, Edward, had himself proclaimed King in his place. Edward, then just eighteen, had become the focus of the Yorkist cause following his father's death during the battle at Wakefield the previous year and Warwick, now the richest nobleman in the land, was his champion. When Edward rode into London at the head of an army of 50,000 knights and men, to the acclaim of the people, Warwick was at his side. For many people in the country Edward represented the hope of better times but for those who remained loyal to King Henry, as did the Bromes and the Catesbys, ahead lay the prospect of being political outcasts: my uncle, William Catesby, joined King Henry in exile in Scotland and Nicholas's father had all his royal appointments taken from him. Cast out of public office, John Brome returned to Baddesley where he had to fight hard to defend his newly acquired properties against the threat of men in favour with the new regime.

One of these men was John Herthill, whose family had long been in dispute with my husband's father over his purchase of the manor of Woodloes, and who was now made Steward to the Earl of Warwick. No doubt Herthill believed that in return for his loyalty to Warwick and the Yorkist cause, the Earl would now support him in securing his acquisition of the Woodloes estates. Nicholas was never exactly sure of the origin of his family's quarrel with Herthill; it probably lay in some dispute over the inheritance of property. He knew that in previous generations both Herthills and Bromes had married into the Mayell family who had held the manor of Woodloes for as long as anyone could remember. But that was in the past, what mattered now was the legal purchase of the property, the deeds and titles, all of which John Brome could readily produce.

It was an uneasy time for the family. It felt as if their father was in disgrace, and yet they knew that he had been a true and trusted servant to the rightful King. Not only that, but he had also served his county, both as a Justice of the Peace and as an MP in the parliaments at Coventry. Now John Brome had to rebuild his reputation. He also had to look for new ways to make money from his estates. He had been the main supplier of beef to the royal household but, with King Henry out of the country, that source of revenue was gone and he needed to look for alternative sources of income.

Much to his own reluctance, Thomas was hastily removed from Warwick Castle and the decision was made that he should now remain close to his father, acting as John's legal assistant and learning all he could from him about business and estate management, as befitted the heir to a family who needed to live on their wits. John and Beatrice were relieved that their eldest daughter, Isabel, was already married to an honest gentleman, Philip Purfrey, who loved Baddesley as they did, and who had already given them their first grandchildren; but they feared for the prospects of their younger daughters, Elizabeth, Agnes and Jocosa, now there was a new royal household and they were out of favour.

Nicholas was pleased to be somewhat remote from the tensions of the family as he continued his lessons in Warwick. His brother, John, soon joined him at Bromesplace and, when not in school, the boys enjoyed their freedom to ride, to practice their sword fighting and archery, and to fish beside the bridge over the Avon. Nicholas was sure he would not get on so well with Thomas. He knew that his elder brother resented giving up his place in Warwick's household and believed that their father should have forgone his allegiance to King Henry when he saw that the Yorkists were likely to gain power.

"If father had been prepared to follow Warwick, he would still have a place in the Exchequer and we would all have the favour of the King," Thomas had once said to him. "But no, he must follow his damned conscience and we are all the worse for it."

23

I know that Nicholas took a completely different view. He greatly admired what his father achieved in those first few difficult years of Edward's reign. Although, to Beatrice's pleasure, John spent more time at Baddesley, he could never remain confined there. He was first and foremost a lawyer and nothing could keep him long from the Temple and the Inns of Court where he carried out his business. He gathered memoranda from witnesses and meticulously documented the evidence supporting his ownership of the properties he had purchased at Baddesley, Woodloes and Lapworth. And, although my own family, the Catesbys, eventually gained Brome Hall in Lapworth, he was successful in retaining the manors of Baddesley and Woodloes. It seemed that the Earl of Warwick was reluctant to be drawn into supporting Herthill's claims to Woodloes after all. Maybe he was aware of the strength of the case John Brome had prepared in defence of his own title to the property or maybe he had other more pressing matters to attend to than the disputes of the Warwickshire gentry.

John proved himself to be as shrewd an estate manager as he was a lawyer. He began renting out his lands for others to farm, which brought him a good income, and he built up the tileworks at Baddesley using local clay and fuel from Hay Wood, so that soon he was able to produce enough tiles to fulfill huge orders. Nicholas told me that the Guild of the Holy Cross in Stratford bought 20,000 tiles to roof their new guildhall, school and arms houses and he always smiled when he saw those buildings and thought of his father's legacy. And the tileworks did not just produce simple tiles for roofing, but also many that were highly glazed and intricately decorated, such as those now beneath my feet on the floor of the church here at Baddesley. I smile to think that John Brome's tiles have become a source of pride for me too: to turn clay into something of such beauty is special indeed.

So, despite being out of favour with the court of the new King Edward IV, my husband's family continued to prosper in a quiet way in Warwickshire and it seemed that even the threat posed by John Herthill had receded. Later Nicholas told me that their father's competence and ability to thrive even in difficult circumstances gave the family a sense of security which must explain why, when visiting London on business, John Brome travelled without escort or bodyguard, taking only Thomas to assist him, to watch and to learn.

My husband's world fell apart one gloomy November day when he was eighteen years of age. John and Thomas were in London, having arrived from Warwickshire the previous evening and, as was their custom, they spent the hours between ten and noon in St. Paul's Walk, catching up with the all the news of the city. The long nave of the cathedral would have been bustling with people and gossip and I have often wondered whether John might have stepped out into the cloister to get a breath of the cold autumn air. If he did, I wonder whether he had any sense of foreboding, whether he felt a chill run through him as he looked at the images of the Dance of Death richly painted there, whether he shivered to see the skeletons of Death, playing their ghastly music, leading all men, princes or paupers, good or wicked, to their doom – and dancing as they did so. I wonder if Lydgate's words filled his mind,

'Death spares neither low nor high degree,
Not Popes or Kings or worthy Emperors.
When they shine most in their prosperity,
He can abate the freshness of their flowers
And darken their bright sun with his showers.'

And whether perhaps he carried those words with him as they made their way down Fleet Street to attend afternoon mass at the church of the White Friars, something they did every day when in London.

The church of the White Friars or Carmelites, close to the River Thames and the Inns of Court, was popular with the lawyers in John Brome's circle and many chose to be buried there in substantial tombs that line the nave amid the towering pillars. The high altar is dedicated to St. Catherine and she looks down upon it and upon the congregation from a fabulous window of coloured glass above, calmly embracing the spiked breaking-wheel upon which it was intended she should die and raising her sword of truth and justice. As I think about that day, I ask St. Catherine, my dearest saint, as I have done so many times before, to intercede with God on my husband's behalf, to set out before Him the details of the events that unfolded before her altar and those that followed later, that He might come to forgive Nicholas and spare him from the pains of Hell.

Thomas assisted with the mass, as he often did, and so was at the altar when John, praying near the back of the church, felt a tug on his sleeve and turned to find a man he vaguely recognised as one of Herthill's servants demanding that he should come outside at once as his master had urgent business with him. Fearing any disturbance during the mass, John quickly left the church to find Herthill lurking in the shadows of the porch, waving a document in his left hand, his face red and blustering. Nicholas was never sure exactly what passed between the two men, presumably some words about the ownership of Woodloes manor, but their exchange was clearly brief, for moments after Thomas saw his father leave the church, he was aware of a commotion around the door and, amidst it, cries for help. Pushing through the crowd, he heard groans of agony from the porch and emerged to see his father slumped below the stone bench, dark blood spilling through his doublet and seeping across the floor. Herthill had thrust a sword upwards between his ribs and deep into his chest before disappearing into the bustle of Fleet Street. A smile crept across Thomas's face as he realised his father's fate, which was shocking to all who saw it. I like to think that smile was an involuntarily response to the sudden horror of the moment but my husband always said it showed that Thomas was glad to see their father suffer for his stubborn refusal to support Warwick and, though I could never believe this to be true, that Thomas was pleased to see their father die, for it meant that he could now take up his inheritance and be free of all control.

John's dying body was dragged back into the church, where many of his fellow lawyers gathered around to hear him dictate his last will with his final breath. He forgave Thomas, his eldest son, for smiling – something my husband could never bring himself to do – and bequeathed to him the manor of Woodloes. Then he expired and a good man, who I truly wish I could have known, was gone.

Everything changed for Nicholas that day. The father who, through his ability and wisdom, had built a place for them in the world had been violently taken from it. And he was dead not by the will of God but by the hand of a despicable rogue. It should not have happened. Death should not have taken him that day. Nicholas felt that now he alone must look after their mother and see to it that their father's interests and estates prospered – for Thomas certainly would not care for them. Suddenly he had to become a man and, for him, manhood meant avenging his father's death, the two were inseparable. On the day that he learned what happened at White Friars, he vowed that Death must take Herthill too.

From that time, Nicholas lived with Beatrice at Baddesley and did all he could to support her. He knew it was right that John Brome should be buried in White Friars Church where he died and, together with his mother, he planned and paid for a substantial tomb to honour his memory. I saw it once when Nicholas took me to London and I believe his father would have found it fitting. Upon it was a Latin inscription that I translated as,

'Lo! Here lies as dust the body of John Brome, a noble and learned man, skilled in the law of the Realm, a child of genius as all Warwick will attest, who fell by the sword in this church, slain at the time of the mass by the hands of wicked men. He was buried in this tomb November 1468. Kindly Father, it is better for him to have eternal rest.'

And I am sure John Brome has indeed found eternal rest, lying as he does in such a solid tomb, his soul raised to Heaven by the prayers of those who read his epitaph and by the substantial achievements of his life: his expertise in the law; his royal service; his lands and manors; his business ventures; his family. As I shiver in the growing cold of the church at Baddesley, I compare his quiet grave with that of my beloved Nicholas, who stands in perpetual agony just feet away from me, suffering still for the consequences of his father's death.

# IV

Even before I married Nicholas, when he was just one man of many in my father's circle who I would hear of from Cousin George or occasionally glimpse arriving at our manor for a court meeting or attending mass on feast days in the church of Corpus Christi in Coventry, I found it hard to reconcile his presence, his upright bearing, his direct and open manner, with the stories that were still told of his impetuous and violent past. It was said that as a young man, he had thought nothing of using his sword against those who crossed him, that on more than one occasion he had murdered to have his revenge and that now, having committed the deadliest of sins, he walked the earth without remorse or regret. Even when he had risen to become Sheriff of Warwickshire and Leicestershire, there were still those who muttered that he had to work hard to keep in check a vicious temper that might erupt again at anytime.

I felt no hint of fear when I was with Nicholas and as I spent time with him and came to know him as a wife, it was still more difficult to conceive of him ever acting without careful thought, let alone using his strength against another. In the early days of our marriage he never spoke about the past, unless it was to refer to some contract drawn up by his father, still cleverly working to the family's advantage, or to a tree in the orchard at Baddesley planted by his mother that continued to produce the tastiest pears. I was curious of course but I had lived long enough in a household of men to know that I would have to bide my time and find just the right moment to slip the matter into conversation if I was to stand any chance of getting him to confide in me.

That did not stop me thinking about his life, though. I considered how he must have felt when his father died in such a sudden and unexpected way. My own father is so dear to me that even after spending many years in his company, I cannot bear the thought of his not being in my life. How very hard it must have been for Nicholas, a young man of just eighteen, to face his father's abrupt departure. John Brome had been everything to his family: his diligence and astuteness had raised the Bromes to a position of influence within the county; his shrewd business transactions and legal practice provided the income to pay for the upkeep of their houses and estates; his love sustained Beatrice and the children. His death must have left a void, an absence which no-one could fill.

It would have been expected that Thomas, as the eldest son, would assume many of his father's duties and take on responsibility for ensuring the Brome's well-being but I do not think it likely that he offered much comfort to his mother or his brothers and sisters. Although I wish it was not so, the smile that curled his lips as he saw his father mortally wounded probably revealed all there was to know about his feelings for his family. Despite this, John's final will was carried out and, as he had wished, Thomas inherited the manor of Woodloes. He lost no time in establishing his own household there, taking Joan Middlemore of Edgbaston as his wife. Nicholas was probably relieved that Thomas made himself scarce from Baddesley. It meant that he did not have to confront the feeling of loathing that swelled in his heart whenever he thought of Thomas. I do not believe that Thomas ever fathered any children, certainly none that lived. His health was always poor and within a year or two he himself was claimed by Death. Some might have forgiven Nicholas if he had seen this as divine justice,

God's punishment of a disloyal son, but in fact I don't think he gave Thomas or his death a moment's thought once it was over. His concern was all for his mother.

Without the presence of an elder brother, it fell on Nicholas to support Beatrice and her younger children. Beatrice withdrew to her rooms at Baddesley and found great solace in her deep faith. A small oak paneled room that opened off her bedroom was established as a private chapel and there she spent her days reading the bible and other religious texts, frequently attended by her private chaplain. The gardens had always been her delight but now she refused even to make her usual short walk to Sunday mass at the parish church, where I now find myself in silent reflection. The path from the manor house to the church is a beautiful one and it might have uplifted her spirits to see the Spring flowers when they came to carpet the woods but that year she did not venture out to see the first snowdrops bravely pushing up their white heads in January, the profusion of golden daffodils in March or the bluebells of early May. Without John she saw no purpose in discussing plans with the gardeners for sowing turnips or pruning apple trees. Nicholas's youngest sister, Jocosa, was their mother's closest companion and support through this difficult time. She too took consolation from reading holy texts and would join her mother in prayers throughout the day. I do not think it was long after this that she entered the priory of Wroxall, a small religious house whose lands adjoin the manor of Baddesley, and took her holy vows. Beatrice commissioned a small statue of her in brass and kept it in her chapel to inspire her own devotions.

It was a great source of comfort to Nicholas to know that these two devout women prayed daily for his father's soul, it freed him to do all he could ensure that the position of the Brome family remained secure, that the assets built up through years of unceasing work were not lost. His world was now full of legal writs and papers, meetings with the bailiff and the steward, and everything he did was to ensure the smooth running of the manor and continued service to his father's clients. The legal training he had gained at his father's side proved invaluable. With Isabella already married and Jocosa deep in prayer, it fell upon his sisters Elizabeth and Agnes to take on their mother's duties in managing the household. There are times when we discover unknown strengths from the turn of fortune's wheel.

The wheel was turning for the whole country at that time and those who had been high were brought low by the treachery of Herthill's master, the Earl of Warwick, whose quest for power had become all consuming. To my husband's disbelief, Warwick took no interest in bringing Herthill to justice for the murder of John Brome, but equally he had no interest in supporting Herthill in his dispute with the Bromes over Woodloes Manor. The Earl had other much more weighty machinations on his mind. Having arranged the marriage of his daughter, Isabel, to King Edward's brother, Clarence, Warwick had the audacity to join Clarence against the King in supporting the Northern rebels. He even held the King captive for a time and attempted to rule the land himself until he realised that the people of England would not recognise his government without the King's authority. Warwick clearly had little time for the petty disputes of his steward and Nicholas was able to keep Woodloes Manor safe.

Warwick continued to stir against King Edward as he had previously done against the exiled King Henry and Nicholas told me that Herthill was later named as one of those who supported him in his rebellion. The year after John Brome's death, Warwick made an alliance with King Henry's wife, Margaret, and the French King. He seemed to use his daughters as pawns in his game and now arranged the marriage of his younger daughter, Anne, to Prince Edward, Henry's heir. How fickle Warwick was in his allegiance! He led forces loyal to Henry in an invasion of England that forced King Edward, the very man he had helped bring to the throne, to flee abroad. Then he had Henry restored as rightful king. It was an amazing turn of fortune. The Lancastrian king who had promoted John Brome to high office was now returned to the throne. Nicholas surely wished that his father had lived to see this reversal and must have felt that it now fell upon him to ensure that the Brome family benefited fully from the new situation in the land.

My husband was a young man at this time, not yet twenty-one. He must have felt deeply the injustice of Herthill escaping unpunished for his father's murder. He could not truly hold his head up as a man while his father's killer went about, freely conducting his business as if he had not taken a life and deprived the world of a true and honest man. Responsibility for doing what was right for the family must have weighed heavily on Nicholas. I know he would have been most anxious to ensure that his father's will was carried out and that meant establishing Woodloes forever as a Brome manor. He must have worried that at some time Herthill, who was clearly a violent man, would renew his claims to the manor, perhaps making some physical attack on the property. I'm sure King Henry's return to the throne and the restored power of the Lancastrians must have given Nicholas the sense that justice could be done and balance restored. He must have felt that fortune now favoured him.

One winter evening – it might have been a year after our marriage – the right moment to talk to Nicholas about these matters came along. After taking dinner with the household at Woodloes, we withdrew to the solar and the warmth of the fire that I had requested to be set there. We often found it restful to sit awhile before bed in quiet conversation. Velvet hangings could be drawn across the windows against the cold and a splendid tapestry further kept out the draughts. The tapestry displayed the arms of the Shirley and Brome families on the background of a field of flowers and had been commissioned by John on his marriage to

Beatrice, a symbol of their union and their love. It had once hung in the great hall at Baddesley and Nicholas brought it with him to Woodloes where it remains to this day, giving me pleasure still. Nicholas was telling me about a young stockman on the estate whose temper had led him to strike a villager who he suspected of stealing a rabbit from the Baddesley warrens.

"We feel things deeply in our youth, husband," I remarked, drawing my heavy gown closer around me, a gown edged with rabbit fur from those very warrens. "Sometimes we act in haste, sure at the time of the righteousness of our cause."

"You are right, Lettice, my dear. When I think of my own actions in youth, it is as if I am looking upon the life of another man altogether." I saw a cloud cross his brow and he turned his face towards the fire. "I have strived to make amends for all I did in those early days, I truly have, you know that."

"I know it. And, has not the Pope himself pardoned you? And the last king too?"

"There is still a shadow, a doubt that nags at me. I pray daily to Almighty God that He too will absolve me."

"But surely, there can be no doubt," I soothed. "Your penance was completed long ago. All is forgiven now."

He shook his head, his gaze fixed firmly in the fire. "You cannot know that. You do not know everything I've done, everything I've thought. And there are some things that perhaps even God cannot bring himself to forgive."

"Tell me, Nicholas, tell me now. You have never spoken to me of what happened at Longbridge and perhaps it may bring some comfort to your soul to unburden yourself to another."

"Ah that… It was so long ago and I remember it as if I am looking at a mummers' play, at an actor on a stage. I had come to find that my every waking moment was filled with thoughts of John Herthill. He had taken away not just my dear father but the honour of our family. I felt that all men were talking of it.

When I walked into a room, others would fall silent and I was sure that they had been talking of the ease with which Herthill had dispensed with John Brome. The best men in London and many who knew my father personally were there in Whitefriars the day my father died. Now in the market place at Warwick, in the manor court, in the guildhall at Stratford, around our estates and in the courts of London, I would hear gossip and whispers of how quickly an upstart family might be brought low. My father had achieved everything through his own hard work and diligence. Without him, the Bromes were thought nothing and there were many who would delight to see us fall."

He paused and I think we both remembered that my own family – Catesby – was one that had stood to benefit from the weakness of the Bromes.

"Or so my young mind believed."

"It was understandable," I sympathized. "He had been everything to you".

"Everything," he agreed. "He was a great man, you know, Lettice, a skilled lawyer, a shrewd businessman. And he was a builder, not just of the great house at Baddesley but of our family. He was constantly working for us – and he was devout. Such a pious man, even at the time of his death he was in prayer. And Herthill chose that very moment to take him from us – there, in a church!

"It shouldn't have happened; it wasn't my father's time to die. I don't know what was said to lure my father out into the porch, but one thing is sure – Herthill did not have the manhood to approach my father himself. Instead he sent one of his men to fetch him out on the pretext of some business. He had not the courage to face John Brome in a fair fight but instead used guile and trickery, the Devil's tools.

"Yes, Herthill had carried out the Devil's work and every day the knowledge grew inside me that I should do all I could to put things right, to see that God's justice was done. I came to believe that Herthill, the man who had caused our pain, should not be allowed to live on, as if nothing were amiss. I came to believe that Herthill should be removed from this world. It was God's will. And of course, I saw that I was the only one who could do it. Thomas was too weak and fickle. He seemed content to hide away at Woodloes and let matters rest. I scorned him." He turned his face towards me now, his eyes ablaze with passion in the light of the fire. "I cursed him. I told him that if he was not man enough to avenge our father's death, then I would take it upon myself to do it.

"How was I to know that Thomas would die, Lettice? How could I have known that within a few weeks my feeble brother would be taken unto God, my curse still ringing in his ears?" He shook his head and turned back to the fire.

"I wonder now whether I am responsible for his death, whether it was my curse that struck him down. But then I just felt my anger against Herthill grow and consume me. I swore an oath to my mother that I would take revenge and restore the good name of the Bromes. I saw Thomas's death as a consequence of my father's and, as Herthill had caused the deaths of two of my family, I came to believe that if I could punish him, if I could kill him, I would be carrying out divine justice. To serve God and my family by one deed: it was a powerful idea."

His eyes held mine, searching for agreement, for reassurance that I would have felt the same. I loved my own father; before I married he had been the whole world to me. My sympathy with Nicholas's loss was heart-felt. I nodded in understanding. But to kill deliberately, to intend to murder, even in revenge, that surely was to commit a deadly sin. I fingered the jeweled pendant, shaped like three sprigs of broom, that he had given me on our wedding day and held it to my chest, keeping my horror closely guarded.

"But how did you manage it, Nicholas?" As the Earl of Warwick's steward, Herthill, must have been well protected by the household men. "Did you act alone?"

"I did. I planned. For weeks I thought of little else. I studied Herthill's movements, the routines of his life. In London I listened carefully to all the talk of the Earl of Warwick and his scheming; people spoke of little else in those days – And then I saw my moment.

"It was winter-time and Warwick was ever absent from his castle, travelling the land to seek support for himself and for King Henry VI, who he had restored once again to the throne. I saw that Herthill rode out each week to the manor court at Barford, where he represented Warwick's interests, and I saw that he rode alone, the manor being a small one and close by. He always set out early, just as the dawn was breaking and took a path over the fields, crossing the Avon at Longbridge. Several times I rode out from Baddesley before dawn and, leaving my horse tethered at a safe distance, I waited in the shadows of the bridge to watch him pass. I noticed that he rode fast, his mount already steaming with exertion as they galloped by.

"There is a point, just beyond the bridge, where the path passes through a small coppice before emerging into Longbridge field. This offered me the cover I required. On the evening before the deed was to be done, I stabled my horse in Warwick and made my way in the growing darkness to the coppice. I had resolved to sleep there through the night to be sure of being in my place, undetected, before the dawn. I had brought some twine with me, thin and grey, which I strung across the path between two small saplings at knee height. I could not sleep, of course, but shivered all night from cold and excitement as I crouched beneath a hawthorn bush, my conscience pricked by its spines.

"Just as the sky in the East began to lighten, the silence of dawn was broken by the sound of distant hooves. I was alert at once, my heart racing. I tested the tautness of the twine. It gave a little as the saplings bent, just as I had intended. I hid myself, standing straight against the trunk of a tall oak just inside the coppice. There was no way that he could know I was there. The thundering of my heart was drowned out by the thundering of the hooves as horse and rider approached. I held myself in tight to the tree, my hand upon the hilt of my sword.

"The cry of the beast was piercing as it fell, its legs pulled from under it, and the cry of the man ripped through the frosty air. Before he could get to his feet, before he could know anything, I was upon him. I grabbed his shoulder and rolled him over. Our eyes met and in that moment, as I plunged my sword into his heart, he recognised me."

Nicholas turned once more to the fire and, seeing that it began to die down, gave the logs a poke with one of the irons kept beside it for the purpose.

"I have never heard a horse make such a noise. It kept up a fearful whinnying as it brought itself on to its knees and eventually stood, shaking its head and snorting as it limped off over the fields. The saplings had done their work and the beast was barely injured, as I had hoped."

His face broke into a brave but uncertain smile as he waited for some response from me. I kept my own face still, holding my shock in check and hugging myself as if I too shivered with the cold.

"And how did you feel, Nicholas? Once it was done."

"As I walked back over the bridge, towards Warwick and the morning, I felt strangely light. I felt the burden of responsibility leave me and I knew that I had honoured my oath to my mother and made my father proud."

"Your heart was at ease?"

"I suppose it was. I felt that everything was right again in the world. Herthill's punishment had been fitting – a sword for a sword and cunning for cunning. Remember I was a young man and possessed all the certainty of youth. In my mind I saw Herthill, dressed in his fine livery, dancing against his will – and beside him danced a skeleton, playing the bagpipes. It was Death leading him away. I saw the Dance of Death and I knew that, for my family, life could now go on.

"That was how I felt then, Lettice. But now, now I find I am not at peace with myself. I wonder if I should have taken my case against Herthill to the law rather than settle it myself. There were many witnesses who would have vouched for the fact that Herthill murdered my father without provocation. I feel certain now that God does not approve of violence, even when motivated by revenge – perhaps still less then. What once seemed honourable to me seems cowardly now, cunning and cowardly. My trickery rendered me no better than Herthill himself, and I deserve no better a death than his. I cannot expect forgiveness, nor should I."

I soothed my husband as best I could, torn between sympathy and horror. That night I did not get to sleep for hours but lay close to my husband thinking over and over the circumstances of Herthill's death as he had told them. My initial shock at learning of the premeditated way Nicholas had set about the thing began to subside as the warmth of his body soothed me. He was no longer that careless young man – and, after all, perhaps it was better that he had not acted recklessly or in the heat of the moment, as I had always assumed. He had been clear about his motive and his intentions, careful in his plans. Above all, he had been true to himself and his family. That could only be good.

Suddenly the church door opens, interrupting my memories of the night when Nicholas shared his burden with me. The parish priest enters, here to prepare the church for the evening mass. I wonder whether Constance and Edward will come to St. James tonight or whether they will hear mass in their private chapel in the manor house. I nod and smile at the priest who has long known me and I move away from the altar steps to give him space.

Soon the bells will be rung to call the faithful to church and I smile as I recall that it was Nicholas who paid for those bells to be cast and, indeed, who paid for the tower to be built in which they hang. I walk down the nave to the bottom of the tower staircase where the bell ropes dangle ready for the peal.

Nicholas never sought to hide the fact that he had killed Herthill. He might have walked away that morning leaving the body in Longbridge field but he was open about his actions and happy to face the consequences. At first it seemed that there would be no punishment. Soon though, Herthill's widow, Elizabeth began to speak out and to stir others against him. Some in the local area took her part but others felt that Nicholas could not be held to blame for righting the wrong that had been done to his family. He told me that, as so often happens in these cases, the matter was finally settled through the arbitration of a group of local gentlemen trusted by both parties. They resolved that both Elizabeth Herthill and Nicholas should make reparation. Elizabeth was required to cease her actions against Nicholas and to pay 100s to the church of St. Mary in Warwick for a priest to say mass for the souls of her husband, John Herthill, and his victim, John Brome, daily for one year, as well as providing bread and wine and wax for the priest's use. For his part Nicholas was instructed to pay her 33s 4d and to ensure that a priest was found to say mass for the souls of the two dead men every day for two years in the church at Baddesley Clinton. I am certain that after the two years had passed, the name of 'Herthill' never again crossed the lips of a priest here at Baddesley, but prayers for my husband's father have continued unceasingly to this day. The priest now lighting the candles and preparing the sacrament will add his voice to the chorus that speeds the soul of John Brome through purgatory.

And so, the matter was laid to rest. Elizabeth Herthill signed a written deed withdrawing all the personal allegations she had ever made against my husband and he felt free of any sense of wrongdoing. He had restored the honour of his family and could now, as his father's heir, concentrate on supporting Beatrice, his younger brother, John, and their sisters, and on furthering the interests of the family. His sense of hearts-ease was such that he soon felt ready to set about finding a wife.

# V

The priest has everything ready in the church. The glow from the few candles on the altar and in the windows makes little impact on the darkness that has now descended on the place, filling the corners and reaching high into the roof of the nave. The light has gone out of the magnificent new window, its figures now somber in the flickering gloom. Bells ring out to summon the faithful to evening mass. Beneath the tiled floor the bones of the dead are waiting.

My mind is now so firmly tied to these past matters that I feel I must stay and add my prayers to those that will soon be said for John Brome – and for my husband too. Wooden pews have recently been installed in the church to provide comfort for all, one of Edward Ferrers innovations particularly welcomed by the older and infirm members of the parish who had previously been forced to find a stone ledge by the wall on which to lean when their legs began to tire. I settle into the obscure darkness of a pew at the back of the church, wishing only to let my memories mingle with my prayers undisturbed.

I never questioned Nicholas about his first wife, so my understanding of her nature, her hopes and her desires comes largely from my tireless imagination. I saw her occasionally, of course. As a very young girl, she and Nicholas were pointed out to me when we found ourselves in company together at the Corpus Christi pageant in Coventry. My girlish mind wove tales around

Nicholas, the murderer, and the mysterious woman who hung upon his arm. Once married, I drew all I could from any hint or passing reference my husband made to Elizabeth. I have given her much thought, yet still I do not feel I know her. She does not lie buried here, that much I am sure of. I do not walk over her bones. She has found a quieter resting place among the graves of her ancestors in a distant parish. Yet, now I find myself in company with her spirit. I want to be close to her. Does she forgive him? Or does she scorn him even in death, ensuring the beetles bore ever deeper into his bones as his soul burns in Hell?

Elizabeth came from the respected and influential Arundel family – that much I know. Her mother, Joan, was married three times, growing wealthier at each husband's demise, and has, I understand, a magnificent tomb in the church of Birtmorton in Worcestershire. For Nicholas, a young man keen to enhance his family's standing following the death of his father and older brother and to ensure his own good reputation after the removal of Herthill, it was a great match. Although only a little older than Nicholas, Elizabeth was already a wealthy widow. The death of her first husband, William Whittington, lord of the manor of Notgrove in Gloucestershire, had left her with two young children and a substantial income. She was also heir to her brother, John Arundel, who as a priest would not himself produce sons to inherit – and the Arundel wealth must have been quite substantial. And there was another attraction, that I imagine must have been as important to Nicholas as her fortune: Elizabeth's family affiliation with the Yorkists and their influence with King Edward, who had by this time been restored to the throne once again after the death of Henry IV, God bless his immortal soul.

John Arundel had the confidence of the King and was soon to become his chaplain. I wonder at the fact that my own husband's brother-in-law heard the confessions of a king! And what desperate confessions they must have been. For it was rumoured that Edward

43

himself gave the order to murder King Henry in the Tower of London, and so took the life of a man who was as close to sainthood as it is possible to be. Henry's death must have been a blow and a sadness to my husband's family, as it was to my own and to all who felt drawn in their hearts to the Lancastrian cause. The Bromes would have shed no tears for the Earl of Warwick, though. He too was dead, slain at the battle of Barnet, but they owed him no loyalty or respect. Nicholas told me he went to look at Warwick's body when it was displayed at St. Paul's and saw that he lay as naked as the day he was born, save for a small scrap of cloth to preserve his modesty. So are the mighty laid low by the turn of fortune's wheel.

Now wishing to put the past aside, Nicholas was wise enough to see that he must move with the times and ally himself with the new King and his supporters. A marriage into the Arundel family would provide him with an opportunity to do just this.

I doubt that Nicholas had even seen Elizabeth when the family began to discuss her as a likely match. Her attractions came in the shape of income from manors in Gloucestershire and contacts at court, not physical beauty or an agreeable nature. I imagine that Beatrice must have emerged from the seclusion of her mourning to enter into the detailed negotiations of the marriage settlement. Perhaps as a mother she wondered whether marriage to a mature woman with children of her own might calm Nicholas, might be a steadying influence. The children, it was decided, would stay at Notgrove in the care of their father's family, as was fitting, and Elizabeth, having already managed a household herself, would bring experience from which Nicholas could only benefit. Her evident fertility was, I assume, a further attraction.

The priest begins to intone the words of the mass. The handful of villagers who have entered the church kneel in silent prayer. The souls of the dead begin to stir.

I notice that Edward Ferrers and Constance are not among the congregation. They must after all be celebrating the evening mass privately with their chaplain. They are such a devoted couple, not just to their faith but also to each other. I think that in this Constance is most unlike her mother.

Elizabeth was not, I think, faithful to Nicholas. Certainly he did not believe her to be so. But when they first married, here in the church porch at Baddesley, his hopes would have been high. I have never heard her spoken of as a beauty; indeed I remember thinking her rather plain when I saw her alongside Nicholas in Coventry. But then, I was just a girl with romantic notions of how a wife should look, much like the young queen with golden hair pulled back from the face into an embroidered cap and a delicate veil enhancing a complexion like alabaster. Despite her padded heart-shaped headdress, once the height of fashion, Elizabeth in her grey gown seemed to me small and inconsequential beside Nicholas's powerful frame, dull against the vivid scarlet and gold of his doublet. I am sure that she offered many attractions to my young husband, though. Having already been a wife, she would not have been shy to undertake her wifely duties and her greater experience in the arts of love must have pleased him greatly. He was always such a vigorous man, overflowing with enthusiasm for physical pursuits. Rich, well connected and good in bed: he must have thought she brought him all he needed.

Their first child came soon: a daughter, Isabel, named for his sister Isabella. Nicholas would have delighted in her and no doubt showered Elizabeth with many gifts and kindnesses. He would have ensured that as his wife and mother to his child, she was well provided for in every way, with maids to attend her person and household men to carry out her instructions when he was away in London. Of course, he would have preferred his first born to be a son, but there was time for many sons, and, I suspect he thought, much sport to be had in the making.

I hear the priest begin to chant the Kyrie, 'Lord have mercy', and I wonder if Nicholas came to love Elizabeth. I think perhaps he did, for he was always so generous with his affection, so open in giving of himself, and consequently, so easily hurt.

There were other children: Johanna, named for his grandmother; Elizabeth, named for his wife; another Johanna as the first had not lived; Cecilia, Maria, Anna – all daughters and all stillborn or dead before they could speak their name. I have seen them recorded in the register of the guild at Knowle. It is the saddest list. My heart is heavy as I think of how Nicholas must have felt, to hold each one in his arms and then to have her slip away. Early glimmers of fear would have led to a growing certainty that God did not look kindly upon his marriage – all girls, and each one too feeble for this world.

Perhaps the seeds of his suspicion began then. Was it likely that children of his would be so frail? Elizabeth, certainly, was small in stature, her frame light and dainty, but he had such a force of life in him. How could it be? He began to look around and see her smile at other men.

I am sure he began to wonder also if perhaps, after all, he was to be punished for taking Herthill's life. He had justified his action perfectly to himself in the past with the knowledge of his honorable intentions: the restoration of his family's good name; justice for his mother; the pursuance of God's will. But what if it had not been God's will, after all? In his heart he began to question his own motives: had he acted out of pride or anger? Both were deadly sins. He could find no rest from these thoughts, no heart's ease. His mother and Jocosa were deeply troubled too and spent many hours on their knees praying for his soul.

He was a good father. Little Isabel, his first born, was a great source of delight to him, I know, and perhaps distracted him from his anxieties for a time, until they returned to gnaw at him. There was nothing he could do to escape God's punishment other than to pray for forgiveness, and that he did daily, fervently. But, what of the possibility that Elizabeth was not faithful to him? That the feeble babes had not been his? He began to watch her as she greeted his guests at dinner, lightly touching their arms as she bent her knees and bowed her head before them; to watch her as she gave her instructions to the household men, brushing her hand against theirs as they turned the pages of the great ledger in which all expenses were recorded or putting her lips to their ears to whisper her instructions so that he might not be disturbed as he dozed by the fireside in the evening. He began to watch her every move. Surely, as a good husband, he should have control of his wife?

In his restlessness, Nicholas would have thrown himself into physical pursuits, riding hard and fast about the countryside, spending hours practicing his archery and swordsmanship and hunting deer on his estates. In the house he could not settle. Elizabeth was with child again and she withdrew from him. He presumed she was fearful of another stillbirth. He saw that she spent her time increasingly in prayer and contemplation. She had arranged for the parish priest to come to the house daily to hear her confession and to guide her in her prayers. He saw them together often; their heads close over her book of hours. He saw her lips redden as she pursed them, pondering the priest's words. He saw her clasped hands tremble as she knelt before the priest and her eyes become dark as they caught his. Perhaps as this played before Nicholas, he felt full of mistrust and uncertainty, not wanting to believe the worst of her. Perhaps he was often from home, finding relief from the weight of his suspicions in the excitement of hunting with hawks or in the thrill of the chase.

I sense the growing restlessness of the dead beneath my feet as they await the climax of the mass and my heart is heavy for Nicholas.

I imagine that one day he returned early from the hunt. The morning had been unsatisfactory from the very start, the young buck he had pursued across the meadows had eluded him in Chase Wood and the dagger he always used to finish off his prey remained

47

dry. His horse had then gone lame near Wroxall and he had chosen to walk the two miles home rather than wait for his groom to fetch another. The early winter air was crisp and his thoughts were of Rhenish wine and a warm fire as he flung open the door of the solar. There he saw them, Elizabeth and the parish priest, she in his arms, her head thrown back as he covered her neck in kisses. Nicholas reacted without thought, he drew his dagger and flung himself at the priest knocking him to the floor and thrusting his blade in deep below the ribs and upwards towards the heart. Only one stab was necessary. As he stepped back, Nicholas felt the blood surge through him pounding in his head and his heart. He spun on his heels and left the room, suddenly aware and fearful of looking at his wife.

Elizabeth fell to her knees before the priest, moaning and sobbing, "No! No! Nicholas, Nicholas, what have you done?" She cradled his head in her arms but it was limp. Blood seeped from the rip in his robe, slowly at first, a dark stain on the black cloth, then faster, streaming to a pool on the floor. "Nicholas. My God! What have you done?" She let his head fall and stood, a gash of red smearing the folds of her dove grey gown. "Nicholas!" She gathered her skirts and ran to find her husband, her dainty slippers splashed with blood. He was in the tower room, the door firmly bolted. She hammered upon it. "Nicholas, husband. You've killed him. The priest is dead. What have you done, husband? Come! Help me, husband."

Inside the tiny room, Nicholas paced, his heart pounding. He daren't open the door for fear of how he might act towards her, what his temper might lead him to. She, his own wife, had betrayed him, had strayed so far from him. How had he not known it? How had he not kept her more close, taken better care? What a poor husband he was that he could not keep his wife. He remembered his earlier feelings of unease. He had sensed that he needed to be more careful of her. He had been vigilant as a good husband should – but she had only been in company with the priest, her confessor, her spiritual guide. He had seen no harm in that – in fact he had encouraged it, taken comfort from her piety and her preference for the company of a priest. Yet all the time, they had been billing and cooing, fawning over each other, when his back was turned. And more, no doubt more, she would have wanted more. God knows what would have gone on if he had not returned home at that moment. In fact, how was he to know that they had not already enjoyed each other? In shock, he heard her cries, her beating on the wooden door. He would not open it. Adultery. It was more than he could bear. And with a priest! The very priest that he had trusted with the care of her soul – and his! Surely she must have the devil in her, to raise the passions of a cold and celibate cleric with the taste of her white neck and yielding lips. She was a temptress skillful enough to inflame a husband to murder.

He remained in the room some hours until Elizabeth had sobbed herself to silence and the wild beating of his heart had given way to empty stillness. In time his mind too was quiet. Having raced with thoughts of her deception, the need to punish her, the outrageousness of her lust, the humiliation that he had not been enough for her, that he had not been a satisfactory husband, that she had needed to look elsewhere; he had come at last to the calm conclusion that the treachery lay entirely with the priest. That man, having chosen a life of celibacy, had betrayed his vows to God and to the people of the parish, had come into another man's house and taken what did not belong to him, what he had no right to have by any law, terrestrial or divine. Nicholas saw that he himself had acted as any gentleman would in defense of his property, realizing his household to be under threat and desiring to protect his unborn child. Yes, certainly the fault lay entirely with the priest and his duplicity. Elizabeth remained his wife and he must look to protect her more securely in the future. He was resolved.

Rather than try to hush the thing up as some men might, perhaps claiming that the priest, most probably suffering from a chill brought on by hours spent kneeling on cold stone, had expired whilst serving his wife the sacrament, Nicholas took every opportunity to tell the world of the priest's violation of his household. Within days the story had spread across the county and reached my childhood home. My father told me he was outraged when he first heard the news. That a priest in whom men put their trust should prove so false! That he should have entered another man's house by stealth, violated another's wife, defiled an unborn child, and sinned against God by breaking his vow of chastity! It was unthinkable. Certainly, they felt that Nicholas Brome should take steps to manage his wife better in the future, but I never heard from them, or any in our neighbourhood, any suggestion that he had not acted perfectly appropriately in killing the priest. He had acted to defend his property: It had been an act of self-defence.

The mass approaches its climax. My lips move with those of the faithful, 'Lamb of God, who takes away the sins of the world, have mercy on us,' but my thoughts are far away in my husband's past.

Despite Nicholas's resolve to place the blame entirely with the priest, I imagine he found it hard to look at his wife. He must have felt both revulsion and disgust at the thought of her and the priest being intimate together and a deep sense of his own lack of worth. It would have hurt him deeply that Elizabeth should choose an emaciated priest, pale in complexion and significance, over him. Physically he recoiled from her and could not bear to touch her.

Elizabeth herself was wise enough to see that she should fall in quietly behind Nicholas's version of events. Protesting her innocence, just as much as mourning the priest or criticizing her husband's violent response, would have suggested that the priest had not taken her by force, damning her and risking her expulsion from the household. So, she remained silent, attending upon her husband's every need, pious and courteous, waiting for the birth of their child and the day when he would reach out to her again.

I know they lost the child, this time a boy, for his name too is recorded in the register of the guild at Knowle: Richard. How desperate my husband must have felt, to lose a son and heir. Surely he must have seen it as God's punishment. I have wondered whether it was at this time that he pondered on how he might attempt to appease God for the deadly sin of murder that he had now twice committed and whether it was then that he came up with the notion that he could be buried standing up. Was he then so full of remorse and fear of damnation that he would make such a terrible pact: forgiveness in exchange for an eternity of being trodden on and scorned by the righteous as they enter God's house?

No, on reflection, I think it was not then. Then, I think, he felt that his terrible grief at his tiny son's death was a just and sufficient punishment that he must bear. In ridding the world of both Herthill and the priest, he had acted as he had to, he had been true to himself and his family, and it was right and proper now that he should accept God's penalty. Then, I believe, he expressed his penance and revealed his love of God through an outpouring of energy and creativity. He looked about the country for ways that he could serve his neighbours at the manor court and the guild. For the beautiful south window of the guild chapel, he commissioned the Brome coat of arms to be made in rich, coloured glass with below it the inscription: 'Pray for the souls of Nicholas Brome, esq. and Elizabeth his wife'.

How many have prayed for his soul, from that day to this? For a moment I cling to the idea that perhaps, if there have been enough who offered up their prayers to God in support of him, his soul might find peace and, despite all that I know, I find myself asking God to forgive him, to spare him the torments of Hell, to bring him peace. My ears become attuned to the incantation of the priest and for a while I find comfort in the words of the mass.

51

Candles flicker in the darkness of the church. Some light the altar before which the priest kneels, others cast their glow over the monuments and brasses in the floor. It is as if their flames quicken the spirits of those below, I feel them reaching out to us, clamouring for our attention, clinging to us and to the hope of salvation we might offer them through our prayers. My thoughts are caught by Beatrice Brome, Nicholas's mother, who stirs beneath the inscription on her chancel stone, 'Here lies Beatrice Brome, a widow, daughter of Ralph Shirley, Knight, formerly wife of John Brome, Esq, of Baddesley Clinton, who died July 10, 1483. May God have mercy on her soul. Amen'. She had spent many hours and days praying for Nicholas after he took revenge on Herthill. Did she live to know that her son had killed again? The date of her death suggests that she might have done, maybe the second murder plunged her into such a state of despair that she lost her will to live. I do not know, for I never spoke to Nicholas of these times, but in my heart I feel the pain of a mother's love for a son; a son who was so considerate, so good and true, so full of life, and yet who she must have believed was surely damned.

Other souls shift deep within the earth as the small congregation makes its response to the priest's intercession, "Deliver us, we beseech Thee, O Lord, from all evils, past, present and to come".

For some time after Nicholas had discovered her sinfulness, he felt repelled by Elizabeth and kept himself from her. It was not so much that he felt a physical revulsion for her, now that she had been defiled, though it had to be admitted that she was growing in years and her body was not as smooth and lithe as formerly. It was more that every time he saw her pure white neck or glimpsed the top of her soft, plump breasts beneath her bodice, the image of the priest sprang into his mind, the priest aroused and smothering her with kisses, devouring her. The picture sickened him and it was weeks before he could steel himself to keep it from his mind and touch her once again.

At least he was now confident in her faithfulness. She behaved as a model wife, solicitous of his needs, respectful. Daily she begged him to forgive her for her infidelity, she had been pressed, she said, the man was a priest after all and Nicholas had to understand that it was hard to resist the seduction of a priest. She knew that Nicholas prayed daily for his own forgiveness, could he not find it in his heart to forgive her? He responded that she should take her appeals to God, for only He could forgive. I know that Nicholas himself could never pardon Elizabeth for her deceit; straightforwardness and open dealings meant everything to him. However, his desperate need for an heir must have spurred him on and after some months she was pregnant again.

Nicholas was delighted at the news of the pregnancy, perhaps thinking it a sign of God's acceptance of his action, but his joy was mixed with a fearfulness that again the child would not live. How could he bear to love and lose another babe? Elizabeth was surely nearing the end of her fertile years and this might be their last hope of a male to hold the Brome estates that he and his father had worked so hard to build. Uncharacteristically, he spent many hours on his knees in communion with God begging for a strong and healthy child, dedicating his whole future life to Christian service.

The birth was a difficult one. Elizabeth seemed to lack the strength she needed and the lives of both mother and child were in jeopardy. Nicholas left the midwife and attendant women to their work and retreated to the small private chapel so beloved of his mother, where he prayed fervently, vowing that he would even excuse Elizabeth her treachery, if only their child should live. The warmth of the oak paneling, the piety of his sister's brass effigy and the comfort of his mother's bible did little to distract him from the cries of agony and each moment was excruciating until Elizabeth fell silent, her moaning ceased, replaced by the high pitched squeal of a baby. Nicholas jumped to his feet as a midwife opened the door and presented him with a tiny bundle swaddled in white linen, "Your daughter, Sir". He pushed back the cloth to see the child's face, pink and perfect and his heart filled to bursting with love. "And Elizabeth?" The good woman shook her head and Nicholas hurried to his wife's bedside. Elizabeth lay exhausted and lifeless. I think he never knew if she heard his words as she slipped away from this world, "I forgive you, wife, for your disloyalty, your indiscretion. It means nothing, I know that now. I forgive you".

Nicholas looked down at the tiny girl still in his arms, "Don't leave me," he whispered. "Don't leave me, stay, please stay". And, despite the pain of her birth and the frailty of the mother who delivered her, she clung to life tenaciously and thrived. As the weeks passed, much to the delight of my husband and his first-born child, Isabel, now ten years old, the baby grew strong and bonny. Together they discussed a name for her and settled on Constance, for of all the offspring Nicholas had fathered since Isabel, she alone remained with them, steadfast and true. She became the apple of her father's eye, doted on by Isabel, and I can well understand their love for her. Constance and I are close in age and temperament and she has become one of my dearest friends.

# VI

In the dying light I look around this beautiful church of St. James at Baddesley and I see so many examples of my husband's goodness, his piety made solid in wood and stone. After Elizabeth died, he committed himself to do good works. God had blessed him with another child, his prayers had been answered and he now set out to do all that he could to repay God's mercy. Even though my husband believed, I think, that he had always acted honorably and that the deaths of Herthill and the priest were justified and acceptable in the eyes of God, he still wanted to do everything possible to make reparation for the sorrows of the past. He vowed to remain celibate and to dedicate his life to the things he loved: his daughters, the Brome lands and manors, and God, his heavenly Father.

The church of St. James in which I now pray would have looked very different at the time Constance was born. Its nave, like many then, was low and dark. My husband brought in light by paying for the walls to be raised and clerestory windows to be installed, the very windows in which our candles burn tonight, illuminating the arching wooden beams with their intricately carved bosses. He had a chancel arch created and a splendid tower built at the west end of the nave, in which were hung three bells to call the faithful to prayer. Nicholas took great interest in every aspect of the work, making all the decisions about craftsmen and designs himself. He chose William Haslewood of Reading to

55

cast the bells as Haslewood had one of the best foundries in the country at that time, and he dedicated them to his name-saint with the inscription, 'Sancte Nicholai, ora pronobis'.

The works he paid for provided employment for many of the young men on his estates, cutting and dragging the ashlar stones from the quarry at Badger's Dell to build the nave and tower, felling timbers in Hay Wood for the roof arches; and there was much skilled work for craftsmen too: stonemasons, carpenters, tilers and glaziers. The improvements took many years to complete and they will last forever: the pride of the people of this parish and a testament to my husband's faith.

In the years immediately after Elizabeth's death, the country was again in turmoil. When King Edward died suddenly, the cause unknown, his brother Richard seized the throne and Edward's young sons, who everyone believed to be safe within the Tower of London, were never glimpsed or heard of again. My cousin, William Catesby, was a great supporter of Richard but he paid the highest price for his loyalty. Just two years into King Richard's reign, Henry Tudor led a great army to invade England and the King fell in the battle of Bosworth Field. Henry ordered that all the lords who had supported Richard should be rounded up and executed. Cousin William was one of those who gave his life for following Richard's cause. For some time afterwards, the name of Catesby was out of favour and my family kept itself quietly at home away from the life of the court. My husband, being a shrewd man, had long suspected that the Catesbys would be weakened by their allegiance to Richard. When the moment came, he took the opportunity to reassert his claim to the Catesby manor at Lapworth that had once been a Brome property. He employed the most learned lawyers to prove his title and succeeded in regaining the estate lost by his family years before. He restored the name, Brome Manor, and took great care to look after its lands and tenants with fairness and diligence.

Around this time also, Nicholas was successful in his dispute with John Herthill's daughter over the ownership of the manor of Woodloes. The beautiful house at Woodloes and all its lands became his and later, together, we made it our family home. My husband took great comfort in the restoration of Brome lands and his confidence began to grow.

The triumph of the new King, Henry VII, brought a fresh start to the country. Henry, a Lancastrian, took pains to unite the country and bring an end at last to the wars and violence between Englishmen by marrying King Edward's daughter, Princess Elizabeth of York. There was a new spirit of reconciliation in the country and this might have been what gave Nicholas the idea of asking the new King to pardon him his past indiscretions. He wrote to Henry requesting a pardon for any crimes he had committed before 1485 when the King's authority began. He did not specify the crimes and I think that many lords at that time were asking for the new King's pardon having supported his rivals in the past. Blanket pardons were common and Nicholas was able to benefit from this. He was able to wipe the slate clean and to have a new beginning. Nicholas also decided that he would write to the Pope in Rome to ask for his forgiveness; although he had made his peace with God, he felt there would be no harm in having the matter clear in black and white. The pardons from the King and the Pope were among Nicholas's most treasured possessions, kept in the strong room at Baddesley, locked in a great coffer hewn from the trunk of a tree. The three locks on the coffer required three keys to open them – one kept by my husband and the other two by his steward and one of his most trusted household men. Soon after we married Nicholas had it opened for me and I saw the documents. I could only marvel that these papers, these very pieces of vellum, were signed and sealed by two of the greatest men who ever lived. With these precious items in his possession, Nicholas was immensely reassured.

My husband's legacy of church building extends beyond the parish here at Baddesley. He took care to improve and beautify the churches on all of his estates. Soon after we were married, we walked together along the lanes to Packwood, where he was keen to show me the changes he had made at the church of St. Giles. The tower there is as beautiful as the one at Baddesley. I have heard some refer to it as 'the Tower of Atonement' and, indeed, part of Nicholas's motivation was to atone for what might be seen as sins, but also he wanted the tower built just for the joy of seeing it reach towards heaven, inspiring all those who came to the church to pray.

We entered through the west door and Nicholas pointed out to me the beautiful stone arch above with its delicately carved bosses, on one side the crowned head of King Henry and on the other, a likeness of the Pope. "As I enter the church I want to be reminded of the pardons I was given," he explained. "I am humble and I want others who enter to think with humility of those two great men and their power to forgive".

The church of St. Giles was dark inside and it took a few moments for our eyes to adjust. The nave was empty, the stone floor, steps and walls cold and silent. Later Edward Ferrers paid for pews to be installed as he did here at in the church at Baddesley, heavy benches cut from oak with curved ends and seats that tip upwards to allow access between the close rows. As the darkness retreated a little and we became used to the gentle light filtering through the panes of the windows high in the nave, a beautiful painting high over the chancel arch became visible. I moved closer to see the detail but Nicholas hung back. It was a Doom painting, the Day of Judgment. In the centre, above the arch, sat God in his Majesty ready to judge all, regardless of their rank in life. Before Him to the left stood people in rich attire, tall, respected: a king with a crown, a bishop with a mitre, lords and ladies; and below them the ranks of the poor: short, emaciated and meanly dressed.

The colours were deep and vivid, crimson, ochre and blue. To the right of the chancel arch everyone was alike in death, rich and poor, respected and despised: all were skeletons now, pale and grey; there were no distinctions, all were equal in death and in the eyes of God as they came before Him. The painters had done their work well and a sense of unease came over me, I offered up prayer for my own forgiveness as well as my husband's and turned back to him.

"The windows you installed allow a wonderful light to fall upon the painting, Nicholas," I said, to distract him from the uncomfortable subject matter. "You have truly enriched the sacred experience of those who pray here." He smiled as I hoped he would and I took his arm and led him back outside into the light.

As one of the new King Henry's loyal followers, my husband had soon become established as a leading member of the gentry in Warwickshire, a true gentleman. He was always busy in his manor courts, and ensuring that the parishes within his estates were run effectively. He set himself to work on the King's behalf and rose to be Sheriff of both Warwickshire and neighbouring Leicestershire. He traveled constantly through both counties carrying out the King's business, settling disputes between neighbours, supporting lords at their manor courts and ensuring that the law was upheld. He became well respected among the leading families of the district, my own included, and was known for his wisdom and fairness.

The time Nicholas devoted to working for the church and the King was matched by the time he spent with his daughters, Isabel and Constance, and they adored him. He loved to read to them from the romances of the time, especially 'Le Mort d'Arthur', written by Thomas Mallory, a Warwickshire lord who had been known to Nicholas's father, John. In Nicholas's own youth, he had heard people speak of these tales of courtly love and about the rich and colourful life Mallory himself led, but as it was recorded in only two or three precious manuscripts, he never read or listened to the tales himself. Now he was able to purchase one of Caxton's wonderful new, printed versions of the work and he enjoyed the stories of Arthur and his knights, their quests, their bravery and their loves, as much as his daughters did. After a busy day at the guildhall in Knowle or Stratford, or riding the lanes of Warwickshire attending to the King's business, he enjoyed coming home to Baddesley and retreating into a different world.

In time, Isabel found a true knight of her own and married him. Thomas Marowe was a sergeant-at-law, whose father, a grocer, had once served as Mayor of London. Nicholas had met Thomas when about his legal business in the City and, impressed by the young man's quick intellect and ability to argue a case with clarity, he invited him to spend some time at Baddesley. He told me that Isabel had loved Thomas dearly and that he had been hopeful that they would produce an heir to secure the future of Baddesley. But it was not to be, Isabel died at her first birthing and the child was a girl, Dorothy. Nicholas opened his heart and home to his granddaughter and she lived as part of the family in Warwickshire while Thomas was about his business in London. Thomas was a good man and a good father to Dorothy. Even when he remarried, he kept a home in Warwickshire so that he could see her often. He remained a loyal and true friend and legal advisor to my husband and Nicholas always held him in high regard.

However, as Nicholas still had no male heirs, the question of the Brome inheritance remained unresolved. He was then unmarried and determined to remain so. But he had worked so hard to secure the Brome properties that I can understand he must have been very concerned to settle the future of Baddesley and his other lands. I think that's why he started to look for a husband for Constance as soon as Isabel died, even though she was still young. I had met Constance several times over the years at celebrations and festivals. Being similar in age, we frequently sought each other out to share confidences. Constance felt anxious about the idea of marriage, she worried about leaving her father and the home they shared at Baddesley, the only home she had ever known. Without a mother to guide her, she was unsure what being a wife entailed. But she was a dutiful daughter and wanted to please her father by following his wishes. Also, she admitted to a thrill of excitement at the prospect of having a household of her own and being paid the respect due to a married woman.

Nicholas looked about among his acquaintance for a suitable match. His work as Sheriff meant that he knew all the leading families in the middle lands of England and this gave him a great advantage when it came to finding the right husband for Constance. After much consideration, he settled on Edward Ferrers. The Ferrers family held extensive lands in the area, their principal property being the manor of Tamworth. Edward was the second son of Sir Henry Ferrers, and as the second son was heir to the family's smaller manor of Fleckloe in Warwickshire. Nicholas probably thought Baddesley with its extensive and productive lands, woods, and quarries, and its moated manor house in delightful gardens, so much more valuable than Fleckloe, would be quite an enticement for the young man, should enticement be needed. He felt confident that the Ferrers family would look favourably on the match and entered into negotiations with Sir Henry.

The marriage settlement was drawn up and Constance and Edward were introduced. There proved no need of enticements. The young couple found that they had much in common, both being strongly attached to their families and devout in their faith. Constance has always lived up to her name; she is such a sweet and loyal friend. I am so happy that she found in Edward a loving soul-mate. The couple proved themselves fertile and within months of the wedding Nicholas was blessed with a grandson, his much longed-for heir.

It was always a joy for me to visit Constance and play with

baby Henry at Baddesley. Although I loved the quiet life I had at home with my father and wished for no other, I found I also took great pleasure from time spent in the company of children. I would often visit my cousin George Catesby and his wife Bess who had a growing brood for me to care for. Over several years through diligence and loyal service, cousin George had restored the honour of the Catesby name lost by his father and worked his way into the favour of King Henry. This achieved, he married the daughter of the King's most intimate advisor and trusted minister, Richard Empson. Cousin Bess was herself a cautious and considerate woman from whom I learned much. In recognition of his fealty, the King restored some of the Catesby wealth to Cousin George and soon after the marriage of Constance and Edward, he approached Nicholas with a request to purchase Brome Manor in Lapworth back from him. Nicholas felt confident enough in his own position to let it go and so, by happy chance, I was able to combine stays with my cousins in their new home with walks along the hedgerows from Lapworth to Baddesley to visit the mother and baby there.

It was a time of much contentment for me and, I wish I could believe, for Nicholas too. His fortunes had turned and he now rode high on the wheel. But I suspect that just as the worm already drills deep into the wood of the pew where I sit, doubt gnawed away at my husband's mind. While his success was now great, it was fragile; chance or a sudden catastrophe might yet bring him low. If God's reckoning could be measured in worldly goods, in wealth and property, in the trust of the King, in well-wishers and future heirs, in pubic buildings and private devotion, then he had been forgiven – and yet? Though my pew is made of the sturdiest oak, on the ground at my feet lie the telltale traces of dust.

# VII

For twenty years after the death of his wife Elizabeth, Nicholas upheld his vow of celibacy – or at least no gossip linking him to any lady reached our quiet corner of Northamptonshire. Certainly Constance never spoke of her father as keeping the company of women. She was always full of praise for his devotion to her and little Henry, as well as to his granddaughter, Dorothy, who he raised with such care and kindness at Baddesley after Isabel's death. I believe he lived the life of a monk for those many years and looked for no other.

That changed the moment he saw Katherine. I learned of their first encounter from my cousin, George, who described it to Father one evening as we sat after dinner, the men enjoying the last of their ale beside the fire and me in a candlelit corner, head bent over my needlework, apparently forgotten. I made a habit of working silently in the evening, enjoying the opportunity it gave me to listen to the conversation of my father and his friends, men's talk. Shut away from the world as I was for much of the time, it was my way of catching up on the news of the county and the concerns of the day. Looking back I see that my position was a privileged one, had I been married or with a mother living, I would have been expected to retreat after dinner with the other ladies to laugh together over a game of cards, discuss the latest fashion for sleeves or muse on where to find the prettiest lace. Instead as my needle flew, I learned what moved the minds and hearts of men.

Katherine Lampet shot an arrow straight through the heart of Nicholas Brome, that was how Cousin George described it and he had it direct from Nicholas himself. He and Nicholas had become neighbours and friends after George had decided to purchase Brome Manor outright to ensure no further dispute. My father continued to insist that money should never have changed hands as the Lapworth manor rightfully belonged to the Catesbys already having been given to them by Nicholas's father back in the reign of Henry VI, God rest his immortal soul, but George said he had been happy to pay to put an end to the matter and to have his growing family settled in the large, moated house. Apparently, Nicholas would occasionally ride there after church on Sunday to share a meal and on his last visit his talk was all of Katherine.

He was in thrall to her, my cousin said. Like a man whose head has been held beneath the water for many minutes and, now released, comes up to take a breath, gulping in the air, heart pounding, Nicholas, deprived of a woman's touch for so many years, found his desire for Katherine was now insatiable.

He had been struck the moment he caught sight of her, a stunning beauty, with lily-white skin and eyes blue as cornflowers – and young too, not yet twenty years. My father's interest was understandably aroused and he demanded to know where Nicholas had found such a flower and whether he had plucked her.

I blushed and bent lower over the embroidery in my lap, relieved that the men were too engrossed to notice me.

Katherine was apparently the sister of two guildsmen from Stratford, Thomas and John Lampet. Nicholas occasionally visited the home of Thomas, on guild business, and on this particular morning, arriving early, he found the sister fetching water from the pump in their yard. Her hair, the colour of corn touched red by the setting sun, streamed loose from an ill-fitting cap, and begged to be touched. "Yes, George", said my father, "You have already established that her beauty is beguiling but what of the family? Who are they?"

"The brothers are good, upstanding men, no doubt. Dyers, both of them, and their business in Stratford thrives," replied my Uncle. "But the family, I think, are nothing notable." Certainly, I had never heard mention of the Lampets. "No, she is nobody," my cousin continued, "But to Nicholas now, she is everything. He says she has the gentlest manners, and when she curtsied to him in welcome, and he saw her bend before him, a fair bloom in the dirt of the yard, he knew he must have her."

"I am sure he did," laughed my father, "Who would not wish to have a young maid who presents her tender breasts before him in the sunshine?"

My heart was beating so hard now that I glanced up, guiltily, sure the men must have noticed me – and even now remembering, here in the church, I feel the thudding of my heart and look around, sure someone must have heard it.

"So has he bedded her? This tender bud from the nondescript earth of Stratford?"

"I rather think not," replied George. "Nicholas says she is as yet untouched by a man and he plans to make her his wife with all haste. He would that she remains pure. It is quite possible that their vows have already been exchanged."

My father shook his head in disbelief. "Marry the maid? When she is not yet twenty and he a man of… What would he be now?"

"He must be half a century and more. Much as I respect the man, I cannot see that he will please her and if he believes he can, he is a deluded fool and an old one too."

I smile as I remember these words, I, who married Nicholas at sixty-one and found him so full of energy and life, his love still strong.

Cousin George was to depart for Lapworth the next day and my interest in what was going on in his corner of Warwickshire was so stirred that by morning I had made my mind up to ask Father if I could perhaps make the journey too and stay awhile with my cousins. I hadn't seen Cousin Bess and the children for many months and I knew the change of scene would refresh me. Father was reluctant at first to let me go, he had come to rely on me not just for company but for the small comforts of life that only a loved one can provide: stockings warmed by the fire on a cool, Spring morning, a hand to rub aching shoulders, freshly gathered primroses brightening the window ledges. But after many assurances that I would make all the necessary arrangements with the servants to provide for his wellbeing, would be gone only two weeks, or three at most, and would return to share all the latest news of Nicholas and the fair Katherine, he agreed to spare me.

We were blessed with fine March weather for our journey, windy but crisp and bright, with soft clouds scudding across the sky and a sense that many things were possible. We rode hard and fast, Cousin George checking regularly that the pace was not too much for me and being continually surprised by my assurances that I was delighted to be in the saddle and loving every moment. A run of frosty nights had hardened the mud on the road, making the going easy. The small market towns of Napton and Southam were soon passed and we picked up the well-worn road that followed the south bank of the River Leam until it merged with the Avon. Across the fields, the towers of Warwick Castle now came into view and drew us on.

The way became busier as we approached, requiring us to slow to a trot. There had clearly been a market that day and we were greeted cordially by many folk as they passed, returning to their farms with empty carts and smiling faces. Beyond the meadows of Myton lay the bridge that would take us across the river and into the town. As we approached, my cousin drew alongside me to point out the hamlet of Bridge End in which stood Bromes Place, the Warwick home of the Brome family for so many years. It was a fine house, beamed and gabled, its ochre walls glowing warmly in the sun. Around it were other substantial houses and cottages, and above it, rising directly from the north bank of the river, soared the grey walls of the castle. It was an imposing sight and I remember thinking that such a view could not help but raise the hopes and ambitions of those who lived with it from day to day.

We rode across the bridge and followed many other travellers, past the small church of St. Nicholas and up Castle Hill towards the high cross where roads from north, south, east and west converged. There we stopped at the Cross Tavern for an hour to rest our horses and revive ourselves with wine and bake-metes.

It was mid-afternoon when we rode out through the North Gate and entered the lanes of Warwickshire once more. The way was narrower now, with high banks on either side. Bare branches of trees reached above us, often meeting overhead to create a tunnel of oak or beech in stark relief against the blue sky and everywhere the grassy banks were carpeted in early spring flowers: a profusion of primroses, but also violets, both blue and white, and dotted amongst them, wood anemones and ladies' slipper. As we passed through Rowington, Cousin George indicated a lane that turned off to the right, leading first through Hay Wood then on to the manor house at Baddesley Clinton.

"Should we make a short detour and see if the family is at home?" suggested George, pulling up his horse. "We could perhaps take some refreshment?"

I dissuaded him, pointing out that Bess and the children would be waiting for us and suggesting that it might be better to visit when we were expected. I also thought, though I did not say it, that I was not looking my best after a day in the saddle wearing old and now mud-splattered riding clothes. The possibility of Nicholas Brome himself seeing me in such a state was enough to make me firm in pressing my cousin to continue on our way. So, we set off again at a canter, crossed Kingsdown Brook, and then slowed our horses to walk the final mile to Brome Manor.

The manor house was warm and inviting that spring afternoon and it felt right for me to be there. A large fire burned in the hearth, Bess welcomed me with a sisterly embrace and the promise of much conversation in the days to come, and the children – all six of them – rushed to greet me, after they had acknowledged their father's return with the appropriate curtseys and bows. The older girls, Margaret and Kate, asked after my father politely and were then eager to know if my dog, Meg, would have pups this year and if she would, could they have two of them as Meg was the sweetest dog in the land. The younger ones, Jane and Audrey, dived under my cloak and fought each other to hold my hand until I pointed out that I had two hands, one for each. William wondered if we had been stopped by robbers on our way and little Richard just hugged my skirts making any further movement difficult. After the quiet of my life at home with Father, it was a delight to be at the centre of this lively family.

Next morning, I sent a manservant with note to Constance to let her know that I would be staying at Brome Manor for the next two weeks and would welcome the chance to meet with her whenever it was convenient. Her answer came by return, she was home that very day and would be most upset if I did not visit her at once. So, at about two o'clock I set off along the lane to Baddesley, retracing on foot our route of the previous day and with fine weather once again. For the best part of an hour I followed the ancient and well-trodden path between the hedgerows. I knew that here I was in the very heart of England, as far from our seacoasts as it was possible to be, and I thought that surely I was surrounded by all that was best and most beautiful in our land. The pretty song of blackbirds, the hawthorn about to break into leaf, lambs in the fields and a clear blue sky – it was a perfect day and my spirits were high as the Baddesley Clinton manor house came into view.

I found Constance by herself. Edward had gone to London on business the previous week and had taken little Henry with him. "I am glad of the peace actually," she confided, and I was not surprised to hear it as I could see at once that she was again with child.

"I am delighted for you," I said, hugging her warmly, "And for Edward. Another little Ferrers! Please give him my warmest congratulations when he returns. And what of your father, is he not at home?"

"No, he is rarely here. He used to spend a lot of time at our house in London or travelling the county on the King's business but lately he has become more involved with the work of the local guilds and is staying at Bromes Place in Warwick."

"And I believe the road from Warwick to Stratford is direct and fast?" I said with a smile.

"Ah, so the news has reached you already? Yes, Father finds many attractions in Stratford at present."

We agreed to take a turn around the gardens and while we did so Constance confided to me her thoughts on the subject of her father's infatuation. From the first, Nicholas had been completely open about his love for Katherine. As soon as he met her, he hurried to tell Constance everything, how she was the most beautiful flower, how her manners were impeccable and how her face lit up when she laughed, brightening his heart too.

"Father told me that her age meant nothing to him, nor his to her. That they met simply as a man and a woman and that without looking for it, love had found them. I can't deny that I'm shocked – she is younger than I am! But I am trying to think things through calmly, her possible motives and his, the likely way their lives might go on – and I'm praying every day that God will reveal His plans to me so that I may see the right way to respond."

"Oh, Constance! You are so good and this must be so hard for you! Why, what motives do you think she has? Is she, perhaps, being encouraged into this by her brothers? Do they look for financial gain or to better themselves and their prospects?"

"I've wondered, but I don't think that is the case at all. By all accounts, the brothers are both successful in their business and have done much to serve their guild, the guild of the Holy Cross. Thomas was even proctor for a time. He's been widowed twice but has just one daughter, who is old enough now to care for herself and look after the house."

"You've made enquiries?"

"I admit I have and I've found that the family is not without money. They are generous in their gifts to the church and Katherine is kept well. I don't think she is a fortune seeker. After all, it was my father who found her as she worked about her brother's house. No, I do not think she looked for this at all.'"

We were walking in the walled garden, our arms linked, enjoying the warmth of the sun that seemed to be trapped there. Early perennials were beginning to push their green shoots through the soil in the beds, promising foxgloves, marigolds and hollyhocks in the months to come.

"But can she really love your father? By that I suppose I mean will she, does she, desire him as a wife must desire her husband if they are to be happy?"

I remember how I felt myself blush as I asked Constance this question. I had called Nicholas to mind, his physical presence as I remembered it and I knew that the answer to my question was certainly 'yes'. I close my eyes now as I kneel in my pew and for a moment I give myself over to the memory of my husband, letting the feeling of his warm and gentle touch embrace me once again.

"I'm sorry but I cannot bring myself to think of that!" Constance replied emphatically. "My father says that she is a true maid, without touch of a man. He says they have already agreed to wed and have exchanged vows privately, so I believe she must return his feelings. He wishes to celebrate the marriage here at

Baddesley as soon as arrangements can be made. He told me he can't bear to wait a moment longer than he must and I wouldn't be surprised to learn that he has already spoken to Robert Banke, our parish priest, to have the banns read this Sunday."

"That soon? How do you feel? Have you spoken to Edward about it?"

"Edward is pleased that Father has not made Katherine his mistress and wishes to celebrate the marriage with reverence and honour before a priest. You know how devout Edward is in his respect for the sacraments! He has always admired Father and this surprise turn of events hasn't shaken his faith in him. He believes that my father must truly be in love. Edward is concerned for us though, for our little family, for Henry and me – and the new baby. He would not like to see Baddesley pass into other hands – the hands of these dyers from Stratford, for example. When he returns from London, Edward plans to thrash things out with Father, and I'm sure an agreement will be reached." She smiled, hopefully. "My two men always seem to see eye-to-eye on business matters".

"But how do you feel about the prospect? A mother nearly ten years your junior?"

"Perhaps it's fortunate that I never knew my own mother, so no-one can threaten to fill her place!" Constance smiled now and relaxed a little. "I suppose I feel that if Edward is happy, and Father is happy, then I should be happy too. And Father is happy! I haven't seen him as lively and jovial for many years. I think perhaps I should cling on to the thought of his present joy and let go my worries about any future consequences. After all he is a wise and wealthy man, what is the worst that could happen?"

We both knew the answer, though neither spoke it: she could break his heart.

The next day the weather changed. Dark clouds rolled in and rain fell heavily, filling the moat around Brome Manor and drenching the few bedraggled ducks that persisted in swimming there. I stayed indoors playing with the children who pestered me to help teach their dogs, Joseph and Jester, some tricks. For some reason, they thought that I must have a way with dogs as my Meg was such a favourite of theirs. I enjoyed their high spirits and was happy to spend time with them. I told Bess I found them all delightful and it was true. I'm sure she thought it was easy for me to say this when I saw them only briefly and didn't have the constant care and trouble of them, but I loved children and it was one of the sharpest sorrows of my life that I had none of my own. Despite Bess's kind encouragement that I might be a mother myself one day, I was sensible enough to know that at nearly thirty, my time had passed.

It was more than a week before the skies brightened and Spring resumed its push. We had word from Baddesley that Nicholas had indeed made arrangements for his marriage to Katherine Lampet, the banns had been read in church and would be repeated again on the next two Sundays, with the celebration set to take place on the first of May. Cousin George pronounced Nicholas 'a lucky man to bed a May Queen at his ripe age'; Bess feigned annoyance and tutted about men not appreciating the good things they had in their own hall and we all agreed that it would be a wonderful thing if we were invited to be present at the wedding.

When some days later a messenger arrived wearing the yellow and green livery of the Bromes, our expectations were high and there was some disappointment in the household when it was found that the note he brought was only from Constance and addressed to me. She requested that I accompany her the following morning for a ride to Stratford with her father. Nicholas wanted her to spend time with Katherine and he planned to take them to Guild Chapel to view for the first time the magnificent wall paintings that had been lately completed there. 'It would give me strength to have you near,' she pleaded. 'Do say you will come'. Intrigued and flattered, I sent by return that it would be my pleasure, though I then fell to fretting over the details of the outing. It took me little time to decide what I would wear: I had brought only two gowns with me from Newnham, so I arranged for the one I was not wearing to be brushed and perfumed, taking comfort from the fact it was my favourite. Other concerns were not so easily dealt with. Nicholas was then Sheriff of Warwickshire and Leicestershire, an important man in the land, with interests far above mine. What could we speak of on the journey? Constance had been so open with me; I knew more of his feelings than was perhaps appropriate. And how should I behave with Katherine? I spent a sleepless night tossing fitfully.

Next morning, though, I was wide-awake and waiting in the stable yard in the cold light of dawn when Nicholas and Constance rode in. My own horse stood ready, his breath steaming, rubbed down and saddled early by my cousin's groom, and I felt ready too now, taking comfort, in the way that women do, from the knowledge that beneath my old and well worn riding cloak, my well-fitting gown was dark midnight blue and dotted with daisies.

It was the first time I met Nicholas Brome. He jumped down from the saddle, flung his reins to the stable lad and strode towards me, reaching out his hands to take mine. I curtseyed before him and felt the warmth of his palms as he raised me up.

"Mistress Catesby, this is a pleasure. I am so glad to learn of your friendship with Constance. I know she enjoys having you staying so close by – and we will both enjoy your company today".

"Thank you, my lord. It is indeed my good fortune to have Constance as a friend." I glanced towards her and we exchanged smiles.

My horse was brought over and Nicholas grasped my waist lifting me easily into the saddle.

"Your father must miss you keenly while you are away from home," he said as he returned to his own horse. "Please give him my regards when you return to Newnham. What is the news from there? My business has kept me very much in these parts of late and it's a long time since I visited Northamptonshire."

We turned our horses out of the yard and I found that the conversation flowed easily and naturally between us. Nicholas and Constance were relaxed in each other's company and in mine. I had worried unnecessarily and the miles passed quickly. Our road through the Forest of Arden was hilly and tree-lined, alive with the song of birds about their spring courtship. It opened out only to pass through Henley, a bustling market town of golden, gabled houses, their jettied upper storeys overhanging the streets. Nicholas was well known here and many people greeted us as we passed. He pointed out some properties he owned in the area and, as we entered the forest once again, amused us with tales of the more unusual misdeeds he had been called upon to deal with as Sheriff. It was an enjoyable time and I had almost forgotten the purpose of our journey when suddenly the road began to descend and we emerged once again from the trees to see valley of the Avon with the spire of the Church of the Holy Trinity and the buildings of Stratford on the horizon.

Nicholas suddenly became anxious saying that he hoped we would approve of his choice of bride. It mattered to him a great deal that Constance should understand how he felt about Katherine. He very much wanted his daughter's good wishes. As we approached the town, his smile became broad and I imagine that he felt the same excitement as a young man would at the prospect of seeing the girl he loved. "You'll love her too, I know it!" he proclaimed. "Once you've seen her, you'll understand."

I remember my first moments with Katherine as well as if they were yesterday. She was stunning. The description of her beauty I had got from Cousin George proved no exaggeration. Her eyes were indeed as blue as cornflowers and her flowing, wavy hair, which she wore loose to her waist, was as golden as the ripening corn itself. My own hair was securely held in place beneath a close-fitting cap that curved around my face and a net that kept the curls neatly in check at the back of my neck. She wore a simple gown of green, cut low and square at the neck and slashed at the sleeves to reveal her fine white chemise. At her neck was a single string of pearls. I at once felt dowdy by comparison; she wore her virginity with delight whereas mine was safely tucked away behind yards of linen and tight-laced dark silk.

Her fingers touched the pearls as she curtsied before Nicholas and I guessed they were a present from him. He kissed her hand lightly and raised her up to introduce her, first to Constance and then to me. She greeted us with warmth and enthusiasm, genuinely pleased to welcome us to her home, and something special happened as she spoke: she made us feel that we were all that mattered in this world, and I saw at once why Nicholas loved her. There was no hesitation about her, the difference between the humble dwelling of her brother, the dyer of Stratford, and the great houses and lands of the Bromes meant nothing to her. Excitedly she led us into the hall where a warm fire blazed and sweetmeats had been set out for us. She was especially solicitous of Nicholas, ensuring that he was comfortably seated in their one chair before proceeding to point out with pride the various furnishings and family trinkets that were of note. There was no artifice about her. She was a self-assured and straightforward young woman, innocent and indisputably in love.

Later, when she knew me better, Katherine confided that at first she had been over-awed by Nicholas's wealth and status, flattered that he should pay her any attention at all. But it was not his power that had seduced her. She could have turned away from the promise of fine clothes and jewels and comfortable houses, but Nicholas himself she could not let go. He was thoughtful and gentle, interested in her family and her brothers' trade, and handsome. She found, quite simply, that she was attracted to him, not as a lord but as a man.

75

So, the question of whether Katherine was a scheming shrew was settled within moments and Constance and I were free to enjoy the rest of our day. Nicholas was in high spirits. I think he had been worried that maybe Katherine would have lost her desire for him in the days since he had last seen her, but finding her constant in her affection, he too could relax.

After our refreshment, we left the Lampets' house and walked along Church Street towards the chapel and the wall paintings we had come to see. Everywhere were signs of the wealth and status of the Guild of the Holy Cross to which Nicholas and the Lampets, together with most of the local gentry, craftsmen and merchants of Stratford, belonged. Along the south side of the street ran first a row of alms houses, each with its arched oak door, then the school house where the sons of the guildsmen were taught Latin and grammar, and beyond that the taller guildhall, a beautiful building of dark brown timbers and ochre plaster with ten leaded windows at street level and many larger ones in the upper storey where meetings and feasts took place. On the corner of the street, where Chapel Lane ran down towards the River Avon, stood the Guild Chapel itself, its newly completed square tower solidly dominating the street.

We turned into the lane and stood a moment to look up and marvel at the four vast windows that filled the east wall and the crenellated roof of the tower high above. Nicholas remarked that so much could be achieved when men came together and recognised their civic and Christian duty to improve this world. I thought of the towers at Baddesley and Packwood that he had raised and asked if he had perhaps been involved in the building of this one. He answered that although he regularly paid money to the Guild of the Holy Cross, this tower and the wonderful decoration we were about to see, had been made possible through the will of a wealthy Stratford mercer, Hugh Clopton, who though he had made his money in London and became that city's mayor, never lost sight of the town that had given him his start in life. "He was a man of vision," Nicholas declared. "We should prepare to be amazed!" Slipping his arm lightly around Katherine's waist and grinning with excitement, he led us through a grand stone porch, watched over by two inscrutable stone angels, and into the nave of the chapel itself.

Immediately we realized that the four huge, arching windows we had admired from the street were matched by four others on the west wall. Light streamed in, filling every corner of the small chapel and illuminating the brightest and most beautiful wall paintings I had ever seen. Other churches that I knew had their Dooms and frescoes, of course, but those images, lit only by candles and what little sun penetrated their small panes and darkened glass, always seemed to me to have an ethereal quality, almost fading away into the gloom. These pictures dazzled.

Hastily we knelt at the small altar offering up our personal prayers, and then moved around the chapel individually, each in silent rapture, taking in all we could of the wondrous sights before us. Huge and richly painted, filling the wall above the chancel arch with vibrant colour was the newly finished Doom, a vivid scene of the Last Judgment, capturing that very moment after death when we will come before God to find whether our future lies in Heaven or in Hell. High above the Cross, in the centre of the painting, richly dressed in a red robe and seated on a rainbow, was our Lord Jesus Christ, his right hand raised in blessing, his left hand, palm down, as if pressing the sinners towards the mouth of Hell. To either side of our Lord knelt the Virgin and St. John: our Lady crowned and wearing a gown of rich blue lined with ermine; St. John bearded and dressed in gold. Sun streamed in through the windows now, illuminating both the blessed and the damned: the blessed on the right being welcomed by St. Peter through the gates of the grand city of Heaven with its towers and turrets and angel musicians; the damned chained together on the left being led by a horned devil through the open, fiery jaws of a giant beast and into the torments of Hell. All the souls were naked, though I noticed with a smile that among those being saved one still had on his crown, another a bishop's hat and several wore bright, red caps.

Yes, I smiled then and was happy, and it seemed to me that Nicholas was smiling too. Although faced directly with the consequences of sin, the naked souls pricked with devil's forks and burnt by flames, he seemed to have no sense of foreboding. He did not hang back as he did after we were married, when we came upon the Doom painting in the church at Packwood. Something must have happened later to shake his confidence, to make him fear the fires of Hell. But on that day, in the Guild Chapel with Katherine, he was sure that he had been pardoned for the actions of his youth and certain of his place in Heaven. I noticed this and felt glad for him.

As I remember it, every wall of the chapel displayed another marvelous painting. Near the altar were detailed depictions of St. George killing the dragon, the murder of St. Thomas a Becket and the decapitation of one king, presumably a pagan from a far off land, by another king, presumably a Christian. Each scene was vividly imagined and captured in bright, joyful colours: blue, red, green and gold; which I thought quite at odds with the violent events portrayed.

The Dance of Death was particularly vibrant, taking up a full sidewall of the nave. In two friezes, one above the other, against a deep, scarlet background, all manner of people successful in this life: a pope, an emperor, a gentlewoman, an astronomer, a minstrel, a merchant; are greeted by the dancing skeleton who is their death. Sometimes he tickles them playfully with a scythe, sometimes nudges with a scroll, sometimes he reaches out to take their hand and always he is smiling. Nicholas joined Katherine at this painting and they spent many minutes discussing it, working out the profession of each character and chuckling over the antics of the skeleton who strikes many wild poses as he dances his jig.

"'The artist who painted this is truly a master of his craft," I heard Nicholas remark. "I think this Death might entice even me to join his dance."

"No!" gasped Katherine, taking his arm. "You must not wish to deprive the world of your presence, Sir. That would be too cruel, for I have only just begun to know you."

My husband beamed at her then, delighted to have found such unexpected love, and I can well imagine how her heart leapt as he bent to brush her cheek with a kiss. I thought how right they looked together: she fair and flushed with the bloom of youth; he dark with greying hair and beard, both neatly clipped, his clothing immaculate. She was a sweet child and led him now to translate for her the Latin of the frieze's final verse, 'Oh, you, my lords and mistresses, who looking for adventure, read this dance...'

Happy to think that Nicholas felt well prepared to meet his maker when his time came, I turned and continued on my own tour of the chapel. One wall was very striking as it depicted the full text of the poem 'Earth upon Earth' with dramatic illustrations. It was a poem I knew well as I had heard my late brother, Robert, recite it long ago and had recorded it in the commonplace book I used to keep as a young girl. It told how man was made of earth and strove through all his days on earth to build something fine, only to finally be buried and become earth once more,

'Earth goes upon earth as mould upon mould
He goes upon earth, glittering like gold,
As if earth never more return to earth should;
And yet shall earth go unto earth faster than he would.'

The painting showed an amazingly down-to-earth-looking angel in a skin tight gold suit decorated with red diamonds and wearing a red cap, calmly holding out his hands and wings above the poem. But for the wings, he could have been a young apprentice from Stratford dressed for a part in a merry mummer's play. This apparent gaiety was in stark contrast to the chilling scene beneath: two men in white knelt beside a grave within which lay a corpse wrapped in a white shroud tied with string, a few white bones and skulls, a white piss-pot and a number of bright red, wriggling worms.

It didn't strike me then, but now as I sit in the failing light of the church at Baddesley, with what remains of my husband beneath the floor, the painting of the contents of a grave still vivid in my mind, I see how there is only earth. Created from earthly desires, nourished by the produce of the earth and finally, laid in the earth to be worked on by worms and other creeping things, we at last become earth – earth to earth, dust to dust. Death dissolves all things.

Nicholas married Katherine in the church porch at Baddesley some two weeks later. Having only lately returned to Newnham, and finding my father anxious for my company, I didn't attend the ceremony. My curiosity had to be content with a second-hand account in a letter from Constance. She described Katherine as looking radiant in a low-waisted gown of gold damask, with gathered sleeves in ivory silk; her sweet face framed by a Spanish cap. It seemed apt to us that she had adopted some of the fashions that her namesake, Princess Katherine, had brought to England from Aragon. At that time there was great sympathy for the princess throughout the land as she mourned her young husband, Prince Arthur, God bless his soul, and few had yet heard the rumours that Arthur's brother, Prince Henry, now wanted her himself. Our Katherine was marrying the most eminent man in Warwickshire and it was fitting that she should dress in the highest style. Constance remarked that she wore no jewels, but came bare necked to the church. Later, at the wedding feast, surrounded by well-wishers, Nicholas presented her with a heavy necklace intricately wrought in gold and studded with sapphires the colour of her eyes.

I have that necklace now, though I have never been able to bring myself to wear it.

Constance did not write just to give me a description of what Katherine wore on their wedding day – interesting as that was to both of us – her main message was that despite any earlier misgivings, she now felt content with her father's match. She had never seen two people happier, she said, and that pleased her. Nicholas had spent so much time alone over the last many years, and he had done so much for others – the church, the guilds, the people of his estates – he deserved companionship and love. More practical arrangements pleased Constance too. Her father had made the manor of Baddesley and the beautiful house at Baddesley Clinton over to her and Edward and had decided to make Woodloes Manor his home with Katherine. Edward Ferrers was apparently delighted with this arrangement, which ensured his family's financial security, and was looking forward to managing his own estates.

I imagine Katherine must have enjoyed living in the manor house at Woodloes as much as I have done. It is a fine old place with a spacious hall and chambers that have been home to many generations and, though it never had a moat like those at Lapworth and Baddesley, it benefits from the delightful gardens and parkland that surround it. The ground is fertile having been cleared from the forest, enclosed and cultivated many years ago, and I have found it possible to grow vegetables and herbs of many kinds, as well as roses and other flowers for the table. Smiling at the way my thoughts have drifted, I realize that gardening would probably not have appealed to a young girl like Katherine and anyway she would have had little time for planning or planting as soon she was with child.

For Nicholas, the birth of his daughter, Elizabeth, was the crowning glory to a year that had seen him serve the King in the highest office as sheriff of the county and marry out of truest and most unexpected love. Any tinge of disappointment he might have felt that this child was not a boy would have dissipated immediately on seeing her. Elizabeth is the fairest and prettiest girl, the image of her mother. I am happy to think of the joy Nicholas must have felt at holding his little daughter, he loved babies and was always so gentle with them, and respectful too. He addressed them as if they could fully comprehend his words, no billing and cooing, he welcomed them straight into his world.

Among the older men of my acquaintance in Northamptonshire, there was much talk of Nicholas Brome and his good fortune. Many envied him and would have enjoyed the attentions of a young wife. My father was of a different view.

"Brome will pay for his pleasure," he pronounced to his friends. "There is nothing worse than the noise and fuss of little children running about the place and with such a young and comely wife, he is doomed to produce a brood of them."

Father was right. Within a year Katherine gave birth to a second child and this time it was the boy Nicholas had been longing and praying for since he was a young man. Constance wrote to me that Nicholas was overjoyed by his tiny son, Edward, and wore a smile on his face from dawn to dusk, 'He feels blessed'.

I ponder those words now, as I sit in my pew, the gloom of the evening engulfing me, 'He feels blessed'. At that time then, he must have believed himself forgiven. He must have been sure that a line had finally been drawn through the sins of his youth; they no longer counted, they had been outweighed. The scales of judgement now tipped in his favour. God had granted him a son and, as proof of His mercy, the son lived and thrived. At that time he enjoyed great good fortune and personal happiness upon this earth and could have had no reason to doubt his redemption.

He felt blessed. How can it be that now he is worse off even than the white-shrouded corpse in the Guild Chapel painting? Red wriggling worms ate the corpse as he lay in his grave. They eat my husband too. Though Nicholas, less fortunate still, does not lie in his grave but, by his own command, stands in the earth of this church forever, facing Hell's torments head on.

I might not have had occasion to be any further involved in the lives of Nicholas and Katherine, had not my cousin George died most unexpectedly just a year or so after they were married. It was a huge loss for our family. George was only just past thirty and his life had held such promise. Father and I knew our own future days would be the poorer for his absence but our immediate thoughts turned to Cousin Bess, left with six small children, all under the age of ten and still living at home. My father felt as much sympathy for her as I did and insisted that I visit Lapworth regularly to provide what support I could. So, to my surprise I found myself spending much of my time surrounded by children. Bess's family were delighted to have me to provide diversion and amusement and I in turn enjoyed their company, teaching the girls how to embroider the flowers we saw in the lanes and meadows and helping the boys, who were younger, to feed the animals being kept for the table: chicks in the yard, fish in the ponds and rabbits in the warren. It was lovely to feel their little hands in mine as we went about our business. Often I would walk over the fields to Baddesley and spend an afternoon with Constance. Edward took his duties as a Christian husband very seriously and Constance seemed to be always with child. They kept a wet nurse at the house as well as two women to care for the older children and the priest, Robert Banke, had begun calling regularly to teach Henry his letters and grammar. Constance was happy and I was pleased for her. Sometimes I would find Katherine also at Baddesley with her babies, Elizabeth and Edward. Her liveliness and laughter always raised my spirits: one moment she would be anxious to learn from

Constance's experience as a mother so she might do her best for her little one; the next she was happy to leave the children with the nursemaids while she collected bluebells in the woods or paddled in the mill pond.

These times were bittersweet for me. The truth was that I would have dearly loved children of my own. I tried to keep that knowledge wrapped in a bundle in my heart, bound closely with twine but occasionally it unraveled and made its way into my mind, pricking me with tears of self-pity: my duty to care for my father and my cousins kept me close to home and I seldom met a man who was not my father's age or someone else's husband.

Whenever I arrived in Warwickshire, Cousin Bess would tell me all the latest happenings in the Brome family. One time there was news that Nicholas's son-in-law, Thomas Marowe, had passed away in London and been buried in St. Botolph's without Bishopsgate in the same vault as his father. With his death Nicholas lost a good lawyer and close companion but it was little Dorothy, then ten years old who felt the loss most keenly. Although her father rarely visited Baddesley, he often sent her letters and presents from the City and had promised that one day he would take her there. Nicholas did all he could to console his grand-daughter and always treated her as well as he would have done her mother, ensuring in his will that she and her heirs were well provided for. On another happier occasion, I learned that Nicholas's sister, Jocosa Joyce, had been made prioress of the small abbey at Wroxall. Although I had never met her, I had always loved her name, thinking that it meant both happiness and joy. Wroxall was just a short walk along the lane from Baddesley but it was a secluded order and once they entered the abbey, the nuns rarely left it. I remember Constance telling me how proud Nicholas was of his sister, how intimate she was with God and how he himself felt closer to Heaven through her mediation.

It was during one of my stays at Lapworth that I learnt that Katherine was in confinement awaiting her third birthing. Some two weeks previously, she had attended mass here in the church of St. James at Baddesley, with the Brome and Ferrers families and their well-wishers, and after hearing their prayers for her safe delivery, she had withdrawn to Woodloes Manor. I thought a lot about Katherine and wondered what was going through her mind as she waited for her time to come. I hoped that she would have good women about her who were experienced in managing childbirth, for she was really still a child herself. An unexpected message from Constance caught me completely by surprise: she suggested that as I was in the county and a close friend, I should join her in attending upon Katherine's labour. I was thrown into a state of some anxiety, even though she reassured me that there were to be other women present too: two of Katherine's ladies and Margaret Hyde, an experienced midwife who had brought Elizabeth and Edward into this world and assisted at the births of all of Constance's babies – by now she had four, all living. Mistress Hyde was thought especially skilled and the fact that she was named Margaret after the patron saint of childbirth was felt most auspicious. Despite having so many cousins, this was my first invitation to be present at a birthing and it was an honour to have been asked, so despite my nerves and my concern that I could be of little practical use, I accepted readily.

Next morning, escorted by one of my cousin's men, I rode out: first to Baddesley to meet Constance and then on with her to Woodloes Manor. At Cousin Bess's suggestion I had with me two pots of honey from the hives at Lapworth, one to soothe the mother and one for the new baby, to prick its appetite. Nicholas must have heard the sound of hooves on cobbles as we arrived in the stable yard as he came out himself to welcome us. He greeted me as warmly as he had done at our first meeting, the day we saw the Doom painting in Stratford.

"Ah, Mistress Catesby, it is a pleasure to see you again." He held out his hands to take mine and I bent in a curtsey before him. "We are grateful to you for coming to assist my wife – and you have not come a moment too soon for I hear from her serving women that her pains have now begun." He turned excitedly to Constance, "My lovely daughter, here and looking so well! Katherine will be so pleased to have you with her now. It is good of you to leave your own family and come to us. All well, I trust?"

"Yes, Father, we are all well. But tell me quickly, has Mistress Hyde been sent for?"

"Indeed she has, and should be here in moments."

He was in good spirits and waved us inside to the hall where ale specially brewed for the occasion and plates of fancy sweets and nuts had been laid out on a long, oak board. Although it was my first time in the house and I would have enjoyed time to look about, Constance was quick to lead us up the well-worn stone staircase to Katherine's chamber, concerned to be sure that all the necessary and appropriate arrangements had been made.

We knocked at the door and waited to be admitted by one of Katherine's ladies, a young woman named Agnes. The chamber for the confinement was the preserve of women only and Agnes was its gatekeeper. Inside the room was darkened, the walls and windows hung with tapestries; the covering at just one small window hooked back to let in a thin shaft of light. Despite the heat of the day, all windows were closed, fresh air being thought injurious to the unborn child. As our eyes adjusted, I saw Katherine seated in a corner where her eyes would not be troubled by the light, in conversation with another of her young ladies, later introduced to us as Anne. As soon as she saw us, Katherine smiled and made to stand but Constance stopped her. "Please stay still and save your energy," she urged. "You'll need it soon enough. Father told us your pains have begun."

Katherine seemed relieved and lowered herself heavily back down to the bench. "Just three so far with many minutes between but thanks be to God, my time is nearly come. I am sick of this room and can't wait a moment longer to get the child out into the world and have my body all to myself again! I know I've done this before but I admit I panicked when I felt the first pain come. Is it the same for you, Constance? Do you sometimes worry about how such a large baby is going to get out? It has to find a way, there is nothing else for it."

Constance sympathized but in a business-like manner. The midwife had not yet arrived, so she looked about the birthing chamber to check that everything was prepared as it should be. The floor was strewn with straw and scented herbs, lavender and rosemary, and many carpets had been layered on it, so we trod softly and quietly as we moved around the room. The bed was heavily draped and comfortably made up with a richly decorated coverlet and many embroidered pillows. On the chest at its foot was a stack of clean linen, neatly folded. There was a good fire burning in the grate which added to the oppressive heat of the room and in front of it had been placed a wooden bath, now empty but with a pail beside it, ready to fetch water when the baby came. In one corner a small table had been set up as an altar with a white cloth, a crucifix, two wooden candlesticks and a bowl of holy water. Constance checked that the water had indeed been blessed by the bishop and was assured that it had. Agnes had settled herself in another corner and was busy tearing linen strips ready to swaddle the baby, winding each one and placing it in a rush basket on the floor beside her. Noticing a small chest beneath the window, upon which had been set various bottles and jars, I crossed the room and added my pots of honey.

"I have heard how reviving a sip of something sweet can be if the labour is long," I explained. "Not that yours will be," I hastened to add. "I am certain of that."

"I am not so sure!" said Katherine. "But I thank you anyway! The honey will be delicious!"

Once Constance had satisfied herself that all the necessary arrangements were in place and the birth was not imminent, we

87

withdrew from the dark and airless chamber, leaving Katherine to the attention of her ladies while we stayed down in the hall below until our assistance was required. Nicholas had gathered some of his well-wishers to support him as he waited for the arrival of his child: the parish priest, his steward and landowners from some of the neighbouring estates. As they enjoyed the ale, their talk was all of King Henry's sickness and how long he might survive it. The latest news from London suggested that he suffered from prolonged bouts of coughing and was becoming progressively weaker. He was never seen in public now. Nicholas remarked that the King had never recovered from the death of his wife when his heart had been broken. There was speculation about young Prince Henry, what sort of king he would make and whether he would have his wish and marry his brother's widow, the Spanish princess Katherine, once his father was gone. It was well known that the Pope had given his dispensation for the marriage to take place, Katherine having sworn that her marriage to prince Arthur had never been consummated. There was some laughter among the men at her assertion that they had never lain together as man and wife and at the Pope's credulity. It was generally felt that when two young people were put together in the marriage bed, the consequences were inevitable.

As always, I enjoyed listening to the talk of the men and would have been happy to pass the evening in this way but calls from Anne in the birthing room above summoned us. Katherine's pains were now strong.

Constance sent a serving girl to meet Mistress Hyde and urge her to hurry and asked Robert Banke to accompany us upstairs to hear Katherine's confession. "It is just a precaution," she assured me. "Everything is sure to be well but whatever happens, it will be best for Katherine to have made her peace with God."

We heard a small groan from within as Agnes opened the chamber door a crack to allow the priest, who as a man was forbidden to enter the room, to pray with her. He knelt on the landing. Beside him the glow of the altar candles within cast a light across the floor. Constance and I withdrew a little to give them privacy. I couldn't imagine that such a lovely young girl as Katherine had much to clear from her conscience but Robert Banke remained at the door a good few minutes intoning the words of the absolution while we, hearing more noises of distress from within, grew impatient to enter.

When we did so, it was clear that the birth pains were intense. Katherine was bent, moaning over the bed, gripping its post. Seeing us enter, she reached out towards Constance and taking her hand made her promise to look after Elizabeth and Edward if she should die. Constance, reassured her with a laugh. 'Why of course, silly lamb, and I hope that you would do the same for me and my children.'

I followed the lead of the other women and used some strips of linen to bind up my hair. Katherine now paced around the room in an agitated state and this pattern of now bending and moaning, now pacing and sighing continued for many minutes until we all felt fit to burst ourselves and were much relieved when the midwife arrived with her bag and birthing stool. Mistress Hyde took control at once, calmly asking Katherine to lie on the bed so that she might feel the baby's position and instructing me to prepare a little honey and vinegar in warm water to be sipped from a small cup made of the blackest jet that she kept in her bag just for this purpose. "Jet has properties that ease the pains of labour," she explained. Constance knelt before the table altar and began to pray for the soul of Katherine and her child and for a safe delivery.

With no experience in the matter of birth, I was hugely shocked to hear the midwife declare that the baby would need turning if it was to find any way into the world. How would that be possible? There was a collective gasp from the other women in the room and Constance crossed herself. Katherine began to sob and I concentrated on my task of giving her sips of the restorative mixture I had prepared and on cooling her forehead with a damp cloth scented with rosewater.

Quickly Mistress Hyde called for linens to be spread on the bed and for Katherine to be moved upon them. From her bag she took a roll of parchment with words upon it, which she spread across Katherine's belly. "A prayer to St. Margaret," she explained. "That she may intercede to make the baby turn and ease its passage." I offered up my own prayer to my special saint then helped in moving Katherine. It took all our strength as she became flustered and resisted us, distraught at the thought of what might be to come. Anne and Agnes held her arms down while I placed pillows behind her head and tried to make her comfortable. The midwife greased her forearm with oil from one of her bottles and with no further ado, thrust her hand inside the writhing girl causing her to cry out in agony, her face contorted. With her other hand she massaged the belly, coaxing the baby to move. Constance left off her praying and hurried to the bedside where she held Katherine's legs apart as Mistress Hyde worked. Katherine let out a fearful howl that must have been heard by all below as the cry of a she-wolf as the baby turned and the midwife withdrew.

With great difficulty we moved Katherine crying and bleeding to the birthing stool, where Anne and Agnes supported her under her arms and Mistress Hyde knelt below urging the girl to push as hard as she might. Constance brought the rosewater and began to rub it into Katherine's thighs to soothe her but she was now alternately sweating and shivering and seemed delirious. The midwife implored her to push harder but she seemed incapable of responding. "Fetch the glass phial of liquid that is wrapped in red velvet in my basket," she commanded me. "It is blessed water brought to me from the shrine of St. Thomas at Canterbury and should rouse her." I passed the precious phial to Constance who chanted the 'Hail Mary' as she touched it to Katherine's lips.

There was a sudden rush of blood and baby and a stench such as I have never known, and the midwife stood with the tiny child in her arms. Anne and Agnes could scarcely support Katherine's weight longer and lowered her to the ground where she writhed and sweated, seemingly not knowing that her baby had arrived.

"Will he live?" I heard Constance ask. Shocked I looked to see if Katherine had heard this but she seemed far away from us, moaning incoherently. Mistress Hyde was silent but took the infant closer to the fire, put her finger in his mouth to clear his throat and then blew gently into his lips several times. She shook her head and the room seemed caught still and silent in that moment. Bending again she blew and instantly a cry issued from the boy. "Yes!" Her voice was full of relief. "He lives, though for how long I can't say. He is weak and if it is God's will, he may not last the night."

"Then he should be christened: you should christen him now!" urged Constance. "The poor mite should not be denied a Christian burial." She hastened out of the chamber to take Nicholas news of his son and find out from him what name they would give him, for Katherine still lay on the floor where Anne held her as she thrashed and mumbled to herself and Agnes used cloths to staunch the flow of blood.

"Surely this cannot be the usual way of things?" I asked the midwife.

"Bless you! No, my dear. Even if a baby lays breach and must be turned, the mother generally has strength to greet her child with open arms. But bleeding such as this? No, this is not nature's usual way."

She passed the babe to Anne who bathed him tenderly and swaddled him in the linen strips that she and Agnes had so hopefully prepared earlier in the day. Constance returned with the news that Nicholas and Katherine had decided on the name 'John' for a boy, in honour of his grandfather, John Brome, and so, as was the custom in such circumstances, Mistress Hyde took the baby to the table altar, dipped her fingers in the bowl of holy water and sprinkled precious droplets on the baby's face and swaddling clothes. As she did so, she recited some words of the Latin rite, casting out the unclean spirit from him and inviting the Holy Spirit to enter. When she ended we joined with her in a sombre and fervent, "Amen". Throughout the short ceremony, John lay unblinking and made no murmur.

"I think I should take him down to meet our father," Constance said with some hesitation. We all agreed that this was the best course, as whatever the outcome, Nicholas should wish to hold his newborn son. The babe was passed gently into her arms and she slipped from the room.

Mistress Hyde then attended to Katherine and urged us to bring her to the bed. The poor girl seemed out of her wits and struggled against us. The midwife took two pots of herbs from her basket, "Dittany and mugwort should work best," and at the table by the window she pounded them together in the small jet bowl, adding a little of the water she had brought from the shrine of St. Thomas Becket in Canterbury to form a pungent paste. Asking Agnes and I to hold Katherine still, she moved to apply it to her belly.

"Can we not let her rest now?" I asked. "Perhaps if we leave her be, she will become calmer and regain her wits."

But Mistress Hyde declared that unless the ebbing away of Katherine's lifeblood could be quelled, she would not be long for this world. Horrified I assisted in the application of the powerful ointment exhorting the poor girl to stay with us. The rubbing of her belly calmed her a little but did nothing to ease the bleeding and within moments she fell into a swoon. Agnes held a bag of aromatic herbs to her nose and then tried pepper to make her sneeze, but she did not revive.

"There must be something more you can do!" I implored.

Mistress Hyde instructed us to loosen Katherine's clothing and take all the pins from her hair. She threw open all the closets, chests and doors in the room, pulled back the tapestries and flung wide the windows. She bent and urgently whispered into Katherine's ear such words as I have never heard before or since, magical words, secret words, words in an unknown tongue. But it was all to no avail. Katherine seemed lost to us.

When Constance returned to the chamber and saw everything in such disarray, light streaming in, she was horrified and demanded that all be restored to darkened stillness. She relit the candles that had been extinguished by sudden blast of air and ordered Anne and Agnes to clear the room of blood-stained rags. Together we washed Katherine and placed clean linens on the bed. We covered her with the beautiful bedspread that had been earlier thrown aside, brushed out her golden hair and made her head comfortable with pillows. She lay quiet now, occasionally mumbling to herself, seemingly unaware of our presence.

Sadly Mistress Hyde mixed a cordial of hemlock and poppy to ease Katherine's pain. She advised us to keep the poor girl comfortable and to get her to take as much of the cordial as we could. Katherine was at the mercy of God's will and she could do no more for her. But being a practical woman, the midwife now saw to the baby, gently giving him honey to suck from her finger and suggesting that Constance send for the wet nurse as soon as possible, for it was clear that Katherine would not be feeding him today. She bustled about her business and I knew it was best never to mention the words that had come from her mouth. In fact, as time passed, I began to doubt that I had heard them at all.

Constance clung to me in shock. Together we stood for a few moments, taking strength from each other, then I gently reminded her that she should go to her father who would be waiting impatiently for news. Far from toasting the boy's safe arrival with his well-wishers, he would now be pacing the boards in the hall below. Soon after she had gone down, we heard a howl of anguish and the heavy thud of boots on the stairs. Nicholas burst into the room without ceremony and rushed to Katherine's side. He took her hand begging her to come back to us. He stroked her hair and lifted her body towards him. She began to struggle and thrash about again and he stepped back in horror. "We must do something! What can we do? There must be something!"

Constance sent out for the wet nurse and for Robert Banke to come from Baddesley with all haste. Later we knelt as the priest sprinkled holy water upon the bed and upon Katherine, offering up the prayer for the anointing of the sick and asking Mary, mother of God, to intercede on her behalf. We prayed together but there was no change in her state. Nicholas stayed at her side all that evening and through the night. She was at times calm, at times writhing, at times quiet, at times moaning incoherently. Next day, she became feverish, the bed drenched in sweat.

Nicholas was distraught. Everything was tried: we cooled her with cloths soaked in the coldest water; we warmed her with a blazing fire; we put bitter herbs on her lips. Nicholas sent to Warwick for a surgeon. "Anything," he said. "Name your price and I will pay it, if only you can save her." An attempt was made to divert the flow of blood by letting it from her ankles but this brought no relief and still her skin burned and her head thrashed from side to side as if she was trying to free some deep thought that would not come loose.

There was nothing more to be done and towards evening of the second day, Constance begged her father to send for the priest again to administer the last rites. He seemed incapable of such a decision, so she summoned Robert Banke herself. Again we gathered and knelt at Katherine's bedside. Before she went into confinement she had received the sacrament of penance and, yesterday, the sacrament of the anointing of the sick. All that remained was the viaticum, the preparation for the last journey, 'For dust thou art, and into dust thou shall return'. I tried to pray calmly, making every word mean something, but it was impossible to suppress the sobs that welled inside me.

Once the prayers were over, we stood, unsure what we should do. Katherine clung on to life, mumbling restlessly. Nicholas, though, seemed calmer now and asked us all to leave the room so that he might say his private goodbye. Constance offered to stay with him but he waved her away saying that he just wanted to be alone with his love one last time. So, we left them and went quietly down to the hall, each with our own sad thoughts. It was only a few minutes later that Nicholas joined us, his face ashen. "She's gone," he said.

John remained in this world just a few days longer than his mother. He didn't take to the wet nurse and we never heard him cry after that one first time. He seemed to simply fade away. His father's heart was already broken.

I grieve for them still.

# VIII

As I look around the church at the others who kneel with me in solemn prayer, I know there is none who has not been touched by death. They mourn parents, friends or even children sadly taken before them, but few I believe have felt grief as keenly as Nicholas did at that time. It tore into him so deeply that he knew not which way to turn and for many days could not make any practical decision, indeed he could not even speak to us but spent all his time alone, closed in his chamber or riding out before the household was awake, heedless of the weather, sparing neither horses nor stable boys.

It was hard to accept that Katherine was gone. When I'd looked at the painting of the Dance of Death, the prancing skeleton reaching out in greeting to men and women of all degrees, I'd imagined Death coming for Nicholas, when all the time it was Katherine he had in his sights. Our happiness is fragile; our brittle bones break.

Katherine had so little time upon this earth. I try to take comfort from the great pleasure I know they had together, but lines from a long-remembered verse now stray into my mind unbidden,

'When the turf is your tower
And your pit is your bower,
The worms then will note
Your skin and white throat.

What help then to thee
Will world's pleasures be?'

I pray for Katherine's sweet soul, that it's journey to Heaven has been swift. For I am sure she is now in the bliss of Heaven, and I try not to picture her as she lays in the earth, but to see her walking in a paradise garden, for she was a beautiful flower, picked just as she came into bloom.

With Nicholas grieving and withdrawn, I felt it right that I should stay for a time at Woodloes Manor. Constance had promised to look after Edward and Elizabeth, but this was hard for her to honour without taking them away with her to Baddesley where her own family needed her. We both felt that it would be devastating for Nicholas to suffer another loss. He may not appear to think about his children as he paced his chamber or travelled aimlessly about the county but he would certainly feel it if they were gone. I wrote to Cousin Bess and my father for their approval and then offered to take on the running of the house and the care of the little ones until Nicholas was strong enough to make other arrangements.

I was used to managing our household at Newnham and took to my duties easily. In the absence of a mistress, the servants were pleased to come to me with their questions and I was happy for them to continue in their usual routines and customs without my interference. For many days, I don't think Nicholas even noticed I was there. He had his food brought to him in his chamber, though much was sent back untouched, and admitted only Robert Banke, who came soon after Katherine's death to pray with Nicholas and offer consolation, but after the first visit even he was turned away. I thanked God daily for Thomas Berkeley, the steward at Woodloes, an experienced man well able to run the estate and deal with the tenants and farmers unsupervised. Without him Nicholas's retreat from the world would have been still more keenly felt.

My intention was to keep everything as it always was, to cause least upset to the children. I found it had been Katherine's custom to take them from the nursery in the early afternoon to walk outdoors if it was a fine day or in the new gallery that stretched across the back of the house if it was raining. I continued this tradition and tried to make our times together happy ones. Edward still had to be carried, which gave plenty of opportunity for me to cuddle him and give him lots of close affection, but Elizabeth, at three years old, was already sturdy and a good little walker. She missed her mother terribly and would sometimes refuse my hugs, pushing me away as I was not the one she wished for. When she did allow me, I would put my arms around her and comfort her as best I could.

On bright, May days we would take Nicholas's dog, Chance, and follow one of the paths through the park that stretched down from the house towards the town of Warwick. Small groups of woodpigeons flew up from the long grass as we passed and occasionally we would spot a buzzard overhead. Elizabeth would do her best to throw sticks for Chance to chase and he delighted in fetching them and laying them at her feet. Her throws were usually short and when she had quickly tired of the game, I would give him more exercise by flinging my sticks into one of the small copses of oaks that littered the park, making him work harder to retrieve them. He was used to accompanying Nicholas as he walked the rounds of his estate and now pined for his master.

When Elizabeth had toddled far enough, we would often make a little camp under the spreading branches of a chestnut tree and while she busied herself collecting flowers to decorate it with, dandelions and daisies, I played with Edward, encouraging him to pull himself up on his little legs or singing rhymes remembered from my own childhood.

Days stretched to weeks. Nicholas removed himself to his London house, writing to Constance that he could no longer abide

Warwickshire. It was a place of continuous pain for him now, offering no possible escape from the finality of his loss but only reminders, reminders everywhere of the sins that had provoked this punishment, his sins. He could not bear it.

"He is wracked with guilt," Robert Banke confided to me. "He thinks these latest deaths are a punishment and he cannot forgive himself." He shook his head. "He says he can never be consoled for the loss of Katherine and John and that he will not have me pray with him again. I believe he feels as much guilt as if he had killed them both himself."

Shocked, my heart reached out to Nicholas in his grief. Strong love sharpens the pain of loss and he had loved Katherine wholeheartedly.

"His thoughts were twisted in agony. You must not mind what he said to you in the immediate pain of their deaths," I assured the priest. "In time he will speak as himself again."

At last a letter arrived from London and it seemed that Nicholas had noticed me after all. He wished to thank me for all that I had done during his present malady and begged that I should remain at Woodloes for some further time as it would much reassure him to know that I was there; indeed he hoped that I would be there still when at last he found the courage to return. After this entreaty, I felt I could do nothing but stay; indeed I wanted nothing more than to stay and look after his children and his household, and to pray that he would soon find comfort from the distress that ravaged him, the distress of a broken heart.

With some prospect at least of Nicholas's return, I threw myself into organizing a complete cleaning of the manor house from top to bottom and was glad to fill my days with practical tasks that occupied my mind: rushes were swept out and replaced with fresh ones mixed with rose petals and mint; stone floors were scrubbed, and carpets and tapestries taken outside and beaten. I even ordered the mattresses to be re-stuffed. The herb garden beside the house was much overgrown – Katherine had not lived to learn the art and pleasure of gardening – but the rampant aromatic plants were perfect to use about the house. We added lavender to the straw in the pillows to induce a good night's sleep and rue to guard against fleas and vermin.

Children's memories are short and, as I stood in for Katherine, her little ones latched on to me. Soon Elizabeth began to speak less of her mother and more about what we would do in the days ahead: would we take grain to feed the ducks in the river by the old mill or look at the beautiful coloured pictures in the books in the library? And Edward took to lifting his arms towards me when he wanted to be picked up for a hug that would comfort us both.

Weeks turned to a month, then two, and it was high summer before Nicholas returned home. By then I had come to love the old stone house with its dark interior, small mullioned windows, and oak-panelled hall. I had taken in hand the gardens, employing two young serving girls to clear the weeds in exchange for my teaching them the names and uses of the medicinal and edible plants. I had found the best pathways around the field edges, where the cow parsley now grew tall and the white dead nettles flowered, to places where I could enjoy views of the hills above Stratford or watch deer in the park beyond Prospect Farm. And of course, I had become greatly attached to everyone in the household, especially the children.

When he arrived back he gave no outward sign that his inner soul was etched with grief. His clothes were newly tailored in London from the best blue velvet; his thick white hair and beard were neatly trimmed and framed a face rosy with health. He greeted me warmly.

"Mistress Catesby, I am most grateful to you, more grateful than I can say. I have presumed upon your kindness far more than I should."

"It has been nothing, Sir. I have been pleased to help you. I have felt so sorry for your loss."

"Please, Mistress Catesby," he held up a hand to stop me from continuing. "Please – may I call you Lettice?" I nodded and smiled my assent. "Please Lettice, do not seek to speak of my suffering, do not try to set things right or comfort me. It cannot be done. I'm a sinner – and that can never be changed."

My face must have shown a flicker of embarrassment at his frankness for he went on quickly, "I tell you this now because I want you to know, and everyone to know, that I have scratched a line through my past. It is over with. It was what it was and I wish never to speak of it. For the future also, I can have no care. I can make no amends, though God knows, I've tried. My punishment will be as it will be. There is no altering it. So, I am resolved to think only of today, of the people here and now. For them there is much I can do and I will take my pleasure from that."

He spoke assuredly, perhaps to convince himself as much as me. This was clearly something he had thought on many times, a speech he had prepared to deliver whenever it was needed, either in company or to himself in private moments. I gathered at once that he wished no talk of Katherine, no words of consolation for his grief. So, being of a practical turn of mind myself, I happily moved to offer him refreshment and suggested that, once replete, he should visit the nursery, where he would find his two delightful cherubs. Later, I proposed, we might take a turn about the grounds, if it would please him, so I might point out the many changes there had been since spring.

I took it upon myself to speak to the household and also to ask Thomas Berkeley to spread the word amongst the tenants and farmers that Nicholas Brome wished no talk of past or future. If they wanted to help him through his time of grief, they were best to keep to matters in hand, to speak only of what was going on today.

101

Constance naturally was quick to visit her father and brought Dorothy with her, a young lady of twelve years now, eager to bring comfort to her grandfather. I was pleased to intercept them before they entered the hall and to explain what I understood of Nicholas's mind.

"I cannot fathom it," Constance mused. "Father has nothing now to be ashamed of. He might have acted impetuously in his youth, but even then only out of a sense of justice, and anyway he has received pardons from King Henry and our Holy Father in Rome. There is nothing he need keep silent about."

"He is still grieving," I explained as much to myself as to Constance and Dorothy, "Perhaps he feels in someway to blame for Katherine's death, and John's. Maybe he believes she was too young, or perhaps that he could have done more to try and save them – brought in a physician sooner perhaps. Who knows? Maybe it is just too painful for him to speak of them."

"Well, if he will not have the past spoken of, then we will respect his wishes, won't we Dorothy?"

"Yes, Aunt Constance. And we will do all we can to cheer him!"

In this way I tried to protect Nicholas from the pain of his thoughts. Whatever his past misdeeds, I believed he had been punished enough. The loss of your love must be the hardest thing in the world to bear – and to lose a son too. My heart ached for Nicholas and I would do all I could to ease his suffering.

There was no mention of my returning to Newnham and I decided not to raise the subject for at least a few days. So, we fell into a routine that suited us both. In the mornings, Nicholas would attend to matters on the manorial estate. He was grateful to Thomas Berkeley for keeping everything running smoothly and rewarded him with a parcel of land out at Woodcote. The tenants were glad to welcome Nicholas back and he took time to talk with each farmer about the quality of their land and the plans they had for it. Meanwhile I continued to oversee the house and gardens as I had done previously and to spend time with Elizabeth and Edward. We would share dinner with the servants in the hall, as was his custom, and then we would withdraw to the gallery. The evenings were warm enough to allow walking or sitting there without need of a fire and the windows offered a fine view of the garden and the hills beyond. Sometimes Thomas Berkeley or an overnight guest would join us, but often we would find ourselves alone.

Given the circumstances, I was surprised how easy our conversation was. Careful to avoid topics that might prompt sad memories, I asked Nicholas about events in London. The old king had died shortly after Katherine and, as had been anticipated, young King Henry had quickly announced that he would marry his brother's widow, Katherine of Aragon. Their coronation had been held while Nicholas was in the City and although he had not the heart to attend the celebrations himself, he was able to relate accounts of the royal procession from the Tower to the Abbey and the magnificent banquet given in Westminster Hall. He reflected on the smooth transition of power to the new king and remembered the skirmishes and battles that had taken place in his youth when the royal succession was not clear and English men had been obliged to take sides and fight against each other. Many evenings spent listening to the fireside talk of my father and his friends had made me well able to engage in discussion with him and comfortable in his company.

One evening as we took turns about the gallery, I asked Nicholas about the changes the young king might make and the impact they would have on the governance of this part of the country. Finding him happy to speculate about the new king's intentions, I was able to ask his views on a matter close to my heart. Just days after news of old King Henry's death had reached us in Warwickshire, my Cousin Bess had written from Lapworth to tell me that her father,

Richard Empson, one of the old king's closest and most trusted advisors, had been arrested and imprisoned. It was another sharp blow for her following so soon after her husband's death and I knew that now was a time she must miss cousin George's support most keenly. I had responded to her with such reassurances as I could think of, suggesting the arrest had been a precautionary measure and that her father was sure to be released once his loyalty to young King Henry had been established. I was anxious to hear Nicholas's thoughts.

"He is flexing his muscles as young men do. Empson has influence and young Henry must make his own show of power to dissuade dissent. I well know how easy it is to act impulsively in youth. Once he feels secure in his position, he will release your kinsman. I'm sure of it."

I remember that as he said this, he paused in his walk and touched my arm in consolation. It was a kind gesture and knowing that he was the one in true need of comfort, my instinct was to reach out to him, to put my arms around him and hold him to me. It seemed the most natural thing but, as was proper, I held back and simply spoke my thanks. His hand lingered only briefly and the moment passed.

One topic of conversation that always brightened Nicholas was the progress of his children and grandchildren. Dorothy he thought a fine maid, and the spitting image of her mother, Isabel. Her parents would be proud to see how she was blossoming. She would make someone a fine wife and Nicholas felt he should soon start looking about for a suitable match. Constance was a joy to him. Of course he had to share her now with her husband but Edward Ferrers was a good man, a devout man who took his responsibilities as a landowner, husband and father most seriously. Their four children were a delight and the stories Constance told of their antics were always a source of amusement. Elizabeth and Edward, he adored. They had grown so much in the few months he was away. Elizabeth could now recite simple rhymes and count to three and Edward was already taking his first steps. Every new achievement was noted and having been witness to them myself, I felt able to share his pride. John we never mentioned.

Although I had begun to feel quite at home at Woodloes, I knew that I should not stay long after Nicholas returned. He made no mention of my leaving but there were people in the county who delighted in gossip and idle talk. I did not want to give them cause to speculate on the relationship of Nicholas Brome, widower, and the unmarried woman who was living in his household. My father, of course, was missing me and there was another concern too. The children were becoming very dear to me, and I to them. The longer I stayed, the more fond we would become of each other and the harder the eventual parting would be. They had already lost their mother. I did not want to be the cause of more pain in their little lives.

I smile now to think that I put these sensible arguments to myself when in reality my heart cried out to stay. I felt the impending loss of the children terribly. I believed that only I could pin up Elizabeth's hair so it would fit neatly beneath her cap; only I could make Edward laugh and open his mouth when he was obstinately refusing to eat. In those few months, I had cared for Woodloes Manor as if it was my home and I had come to love the place. Then of course, there was Nicholas himself, so easy to be with. I knew the great effort he was making to engage again with life and I wanted nothing more than to be there to support him.

I remember that in the end I made my excuses and retreated from Woodloes quite hurriedly. It was the only way I could manage it. Back at Father's house in Northamptonshire, I attempted to resume my previous quiet life. Our home at Newnham was much smaller than Woodloes and easily maintained by family servants who had been with us for many years. Father was very pleased to have me home but my arrival did little to alter the slow pace of his days. Other than the expectation of some long walks through the meadows with Meg, who had welcomed me back with an enthusiastic wagging tail, there was little to divert me. With so much time to ponder life, a deep regret filled my heart, the regret of having no one to share my time with and no children of my own. I had to work hard to resist becoming maudlin and some days I just gave in to sobbing privately: I would never feel a little hand in mine and hear someone call me 'Mother'; I would never turn to a husband for comfort as evening fell.

It was just days before the first letter from Nicholas arrived. He inquired after my health, hoped I had found my father well and reported that he had taken the children to pick the first ripe apple from a pippin tree that very morning. Naturally, I replied swiftly, wishing nothing more than to send my love to Elizabeth and Edward and my best wishes to all at the manor. Soon a regular correspondence struck up between us. It was an unlooked-for joy and kept me from falling into a deep despondency that autumn.

Nicholas's letters contained news of the minutiae of daily life, trivial snippets really, but they kept my memories of Woodloes alive. He wrote with a bold hand, more used to recording jury verdicts or accounts of tithes paid, but he seemed happy to share with me details of the children's latest achievements or the harvest from the vegetable garden. These were the things he knew would interest me. I was so glad that my father had allowed me to join my brothers' early lessons with their tutor; as a result I had developed handwriting that was passable for a woman, legible and clear. Some ladies I knew had to rely upon dictating to their clerk or a male member of their family when they wished to send a letter and I was happy not to have that inhibition. I was free to write what was in my mind without constraint.

The three sprigs of yellow and green of the Brome livery became a common sight in our Northamptonshire lanes at that time. It puzzled my father to have letters arriving almost daily and he probably begrudged the expense of my sending to Warwick for more paper, though he restrained himself from mentioning it. It was nearly a full day's ride from Newnham to Woodloes Manor and back and we could not spare a man to make the journey regularly, so often I would have a letter ready to return with Nicholas's messenger, asking him to wait while I hurriedly broke the red wax seal on Nicholas's letter and skimmed through his words before adding a few extra lines to my own in response. Once the rider and horse had been fed and watered and were on their way back, I would retire to my chamber to pour over every detail Nicholas had written. He would always fold his paper twice, securing it with thread and adding his distinctive seal stamped with the mark of a single tree. On the outside the letters were addressed to 'Mistress Catesby' but within he always wrote to 'My Dear Lettice'.

Perhaps I should not have been surprised when one gloomy November morning, two sets of horses hooves clattered into our cobbled stable yard and Nicholas himself arrived escorted by the familiar messenger. I already knew him to be a man more disposed to action than to words and probably my astonishment should have been that he would write so many letters. I was surprised though, and totally caught off my guard when he made his proposal to me. He wanted me to return to Woodloes. The children needed me, he said. They asked for me every day. The place was not the same without me. It was cold; it was dreary. The heart had gone out of it and without me there, he could see no prospect of it returning again to warmth and life. The children should not have to grow up without a woman's love and yet he could not bear to send them away to be raised by others.

"My dear Lettice, I speak of the children but indeed I find that I am in dire need of you myself. I beg you to come back to Woodloes Manor – and to come not as my well-wisher but as my wife."

"But what about Katherine?' I blurted in shock. 'She has been dead only half a year, or less. Surely…"

"We will not speak of her," he interrupted firmly. Seeing my concern he continued in more measured tones, "I cannot speak of her, Lettice, it would undo me. Please understand and accept it, for my deepest wish is to go on in life with you beside me."

As I remained silent, he continued, "I see this comes as a great surprise to you. So, I will leave you now to consider how you feel in the matter. I ask you only to know that my regard and fondness for you is true and that, should you consent to be my companion and my wife, I fully intend to do all I can to make our days together pleasurable."

He left me then, as suddenly as he had arrived, urging me with a hopeful, boyish grin to write to him as soon as I had my answer.

Looking back now, I remember how Nicholas's proposal threw me into an agony of indecision. I managed to come up with countless reasons against accepting him. Nicholas was so much older than me: twenty-five years, which was more than a lifetime for many; his experience was so much beyond mine: how would we possibly relate to each other? And yet he seemed to enjoy conversing with me and to respect and value me as an equal. At some time in the future, perhaps not so very distant, he would be a frail, old man: I might, perhaps, have to nurse him through illness and worse; how would I feel if I had to devote my days to the care of a decrepit invalid? And yet this was already an inevitable prospect for me as the alternative I faced was to stay home and nurse my father- and anyway, Nicholas was so vigorous and full of energy. It was too soon after Katherine's death: people would talk about Nicholas being inconstant and me, well, they would be bound to see me as a scheming spinster who had inveigled my way into his life when he was at his lowest ebb and now meant to benefit from his generosity. And yet my heart yearned to be back at the manor house I loved with the children – and with him.

In the end it was a long talk with my father that resolved the matter. I had expected his opposition but he was surprisingly positive about the prospect of my marrying Nicholas Brome. He saw the matter primarily as a business transaction rather than an affair of the heart. Now that the matter of the ownership of Lapworth Manor had been resolved and the Catesbys safely settled there, he felt that a marriage union with the Bromes would only serve to strengthen the accord and further establish the presence of our family in the area. He was rather impressed that I had managed to catch the eye of a man like Nicholas Brome – though he was quick to reassure me that of course I deserved no less a man – and pointed out that my future security would be assured if I were to marry one of the most prominent esquires in Warwickshire. Father might have had an eye to the future security of our affairs but he was also a compassionate man. I had told him much about Elizabeth and Edward and my great fondness for them. He had come to care about them too and was sorry to think of them growing up without a mother's love. He knew that I would bring a great deal of joy to their young lives and he had a sincere concern for my future wellbeing too. He assured me that he had never thought to have me always with him and that he would be very content to pass his days quietly at Newnham with his servants and friends around him, if he could picture me as mistress of my own household and know that I was happy.

So it was that a week after the unexpected proposal, I put my quill to paper once again and wrote to Nicholas that I would marry him. My father did not resent the sending of a special messenger to Woodloes Manor and by return I received Nicholas's delighted response. 'My dearest Lettice,' he wrote. 'Today I am the happiest man in England and I promise you will never regret your kind decision, for my only intention from this day on is to ensure your heart's ease.' With the letter he sent a single rose, one of the last of the season's blooms, that took my mind back to June in the delightful gardens at Woodloes and led my heart on to a tremulous place where it had never been.

Some days are etched vividly into my mind, each detail standing out in sharp relief. My wedding day is one of these, the memory of it still bright and clear to me now some seventeen years later.

We were married in the church porch at Baddesley Clinton on the first day of January 1510. There had been no reason to delay beyond the three Sundays needed for the banns to be read, and the first day of a new year seemed an auspicious one for such a ceremony. It was a cold, crisp morning with a hoar frost in the fields and the hedges decorated with icy spiders' webs. A large group of well-wishers waited for me as I walked the short oak-lined path from the manor house beneath the bare, arching branches, on the arm of my father, proudly sporting his warmest gown of black velvet lined with fur. We were accompanied by Constance who, much to my relief, had declared herself delighted with the match and professed always to have known we two should be kinswomen. The guests huddled around the church door included our closest family: my brother, Thomas Catesby; Bess and the children from Lapworth; Nicholas's brother, John Brome; Edward Ferrers; and the Ferrers children and Dorothy, who I smiled to realise would now become my step-grandchildren. Several of the local gentry were in attendance, keen to give Nicholas their support, and Thomas Berkeley, together with many servants and tenants from Woodloes, had walked across the fields that morning to offer us their blessing.

I wore a gown of white brocade shot through with silks of scarlet, green and gold and trimmed at the hem with ermine. On my shoulders lay a scarlet cloak of heavy velvet secured with an intricately wrought gold clasp; and around my neck hung the jewelled pendant shaped like three sprigs of broom that Nicholas had given me to wear upon our wedding day. He had insisted that I send to London for the best fabrics, and the finest seamstress in Warwick had been employed throughout the Christmas-time to make my wedding clothes. Remembering the impression Katherine's flowing golden tresses had made on me the first time I ever saw her, I wore my dark hair loose that day, brushed to a shine and held in place with a simple band of wide velvet ribbon, in a green to complement my eyes. Never before had I taken such care or delight in my appearance and I admit to feeling more than a little self conscious as I approached the gathering. Perhaps sensing my nervousness, Nicholas stepped from the group to join me and taking my arm gently from my father's led me the final steps to the porch where Robert Banke, missal in hand, met us solemnly and began the sacrament.

"Do you Nicholas Brome take Letitia Catesby to be your wife?"

"I do," Nicholas replied firmly.

"Do you Letitia Catesby take Nicholas Brome to be your husband?"

Determined to remain composed, I responded with equal assurance, "I do."

Robert Banke then held out his book, richly bound and gilded, and Nicholas placed upon it a red-gold ruby ring together with two bright, gold coins.

The priest took my left hand as he blessed the ring, "In nomina Patrice et Fili et Spiritu Santi," and, as all joined in the 'Amen', he slipped the coins into his pocket, the ring onto my fourth finger and I was married to Nicholas Brome.

However, the ceremony was not yet over. The door to the church was opened and the priest led us inside, followed by our well-wishers. I am glad I had no inkling then that my husband would one day be buried inside that same door for all to tread upon or that I would one day sit in that same church praying for his soul and anguishing over his salvation. Nicholas never let it show in his face but I know he was sure in his heart even then that he would find no eternal rest. In marrying me he chose to take what happiness in life remained to him.

As we approached the altar step, the priest began his psalms, songs of the sanctity and fecundity of marriage, and all around I saw that the church had been decorated with evergreens, with holly and ivy and hawthorn berries, signs that life clung on through the winter cold and that the hedgerows would soon burst into life again. I glanced at my husband's face, his glowing skin, his shining white hair, and sensing my gaze, he caught my eye with the twinkle of a smile. We knelt before the priest and prayers were said over us, prayers to the glory of God whose love had brought us together and now bound us in a bond, unbreakable while we both should live.

We then took the final step up to the altar and lay ourselves face down upon the tiles, the same rich red, decorated tiles that lie now beneath my feet. I remember feeling them cold against my cheek. My brother, Thomas, and Nicholas's brother, John, then stepped forward, together with Edward and Constance, and each took a corner of the wedding veil. They held it over us while the priest blessed our union and the future offspring of it. When all prayers were said and the peace of God was upon us, and the gathered congregation, the priest offered his hand to Nicholas, raised him up and kissed him on the cheek to seal the bond. Nicholas in turn helped me to my feet, and then kissed me long and soft upon my lips. It was the first time I had been kissed so by a man and it was my wedding day. My heart leapt and my face broke into a smile that remained in place all the way down the aisle, as Nicholas led me through the nods and greetings of our family and friends, and out into the pale sunshine of the January morning.

Indeed that smile is with me still, as I think back to our happiness that day and the brief, unexpected joy we found together.

Constance had arranged a wedding feast for us in the great hall at Baddesley and we made our way there arm in arm at the head of the straggling procession of family and friends. With every breath,

I felt the crisp, winter air reach into me. With every move of my left hand, I felt the unusual constraint of the ring upon my finger. Both sensations were exhilarating. In the hall we found torches and candles already lit, the board spread with all manner of tasty dishes, silver goblets and jugs of Burgundy wine, and placed at its head, two heavy oak chairs laced with garlands of greenery. We took our seats and enjoyed a day of merriment.

It was good that much wine flowed and that when the feast was finally over, I became caught up in the music and dancing, for it meant I felt only surprise when Constance tapped me on the arm and suggested that it was time for us to go up and prepare the marriage bed. Had I not been so relaxed, I might have been overcome with anxiety about exactly what was to happen in the night ahead; for certainly my mind had been concerned with little else in the preceding days. As I had no clear idea of what might be expected of me, would I understand what I should do when the time came? Would the disparity in our experience mean I would disappoint him? Would he be gentle? Would there be pain? Or would there be no contact between us? Was he marrying me for companionship only? And if so, would I be disappointed or relieved?

But the red grape had done its work, and no such thoughts entered my mind as I went laughingly with Constance and the other ladies to a chamber they had already decked with gold and silver silks, sparkling now in the candlelight. The bed was strewn with dried rose petals and lavender, there being no fresh blooms to be had in winter, and upon it was spread a chemise of the palest, lightest, whitest silk. I held my arms above my head for the ladies to remove my tight-laced wedding clothes and slip on this gown of gossamer, so cool and soft against my skin. I shivered with goosebumps despite the glowing fire and was helped willingly, barefoot, into bed.

Sliding between the cool linen sheets cleared my mind a little. I became aware of the noise of music and laughter from the party still continuing below and began to remember tales my father and brothers had told me of the carousing of men as they escorted husbands to the marriage bed, the lewdness of their drunken comments. I lay as if frozen as I heard footsteps approaching and was much relieved when the door opened and Nicholas alone stepped into the chamber. The ladies bowed their heads and took their leave quickly, Constance catching her father's eye as she passed, and the door closed behind them.

Nicholas seemed a little ill at ease himself as he sat at the bottom corner of the bed and spoke without looking at me.

"I hope you don't mind me breaking with tradition and coming to you unaccompanied. In truth I am too old for the high-spirited teasing of young bucks. They mean well but there really is no need. I've heard it all before and need no encouragement to enjoy the delights of the marriage bed."

I lay still and silent, my eyes on the delicate needlework of the hanging above me.

"But I hope *you* are not disappointed to miss their revelry?"

"I am not, Sir," I whispered nervously.

"Why, Lettice, my dear, you are shivering!"

He turned to me with concern and touched my fingers where they gripped the coverlet. "The room has not been made warm enough. I'll stoke the fire."

"No, my lord – Nicholas," I held his hand to prevent his moving away. "It is not that. I am not cold. I fear it is wedding nerves that make me shiver. I so want to make you happy but I…"

He interrupted by putting his mouth to mine and kissing me with such lingering gentleness that I felt my body thaw and move to meet him. No further words were spoken, and by the time he had made me smile by awkwardly trying to remove his clothes without breaking from our embrace and then slipped naked under the covers to join me, the wine was lulling me again and I lost myself to the warm urgency of his touch and the thrill of my response.

114

In my innocence I did not think to doubt Nicholas's wisdom in coming to me alone that night. It took Edward and Constance to point out to us the folly of his 'creeping away' from the wedding feast.

"I can understand you wanting to avoid the public spectacle, Sir, but by shirking the whole 'putting to bed' ritual, you omitted to invite the priest to bless the marriage bed," Edward pointed out.

"Reverend Banke was most concerned by your behavior," added Constance. "I fear for your soul, Father, I do. There are times when you really seem to think only of your pleasure in this earthly life and to care not a jot for the hereafter."

"Nothing could be further from the truth, I do assure you," Nicholas replied quietly.

Sensing they had hit upon a seam of deep sorrow in him, I quickly thought what could be done to resolve the matter.

"Why don't we ask Reverend Banke to attend us at Woodloes later in the day?" I suggested. "After all, Woodloes is where our true marriage bed awaits us. Baddesley Clinton was just a temporary lodging where we rested the night as your guests."

"That's right," agreed Nicholas, brightening. "I'll arrange for a priest to call on us at Woodloes before evening. You may rest assured, my dear children, by nightfall our marriage bed will have been blessed in accordance with the rituals of the church as is right and proper."

We had our horses saddled then and, restored to high spirits, left for the short ride to Woodloes Manor; the house where we would be happy, the home that I love still.

As we trotted amiably together, I asked Nicholas whether he thought the matter of our un-blessed marriage bed should trouble us at all.

"Give no further thought to it, Lettice," he said. "You are the most modest and chaste of women. Your purity on our wedding night was known to God." He brought his horse to a stop and reached to take and kiss my hand. "Assuredly you will find your place in Heaven." He looked into my eyes to be sure I was listening well to him. "Of my soul, I prefer us never to speak."

"But shall we send for Reverend Banke?"

"No, my dear, I will see no more of Banke. To please my daughter and son-in-law in their piety, I agreed for him to marry us at Baddesley but I wish no further dealings with him."

"Why, Nicholas, has he upset you in some way?" I asked, remembering my conversation with the priest soon after Katherine's death.

"It's all past, my dear. Let's leave it there and look to the future. If you wish our bed at Woodloes to be blessed, we'll send for a priest from Warwick to get the thing done."

"I think I would prefer it."

"Then that is what we will do.'" He gave me a warm smile. "My wish is to please you, Lettice. For I have more than I deserve in this chance of happiness with you."

That afternoon, with a priest from St. Nicholas Church in Warwick summoned, I asked for the servants' help in finding the richest fabrics in the house's coffers to decorate the best bedchamber. There was little to be picked in the kitchen garden in January, but the rosemary clung on and I followed Constance's example by adding to it dried lavender and rose petals to sprinkle over the bed. By the time the priest arrived all was prepared as it should be and together we welcomed him and accompanied him to the marriage bed.

We did not lay upon the bed in his presence, as was the custom, it no longer seemed fitting, but stood beside it, hands clasped, as he offered up his solemn prayer,

"Bless O Lord this marriage bed and those who lie in it that they may live in your love and multiply and grow old together."

Then he left us, closing the door softly behind him, and we turned to each other.

Any one who thinks a man of sixty well past his prime is much mistaken. Nicholas lived life to the full and delighted in its present pleasures. The next years were my happiest.

Far from retreating from public life as many had thought he might after Katherine's death, he threw himself into the service of the new, young King. He wanted Henry to be secure in his power and the country prosperous, so he accepted the position of the King's Escheator for Warwickshire and Leicestershire. His duty was to seek out those likely to die intestate, whose lands might therefore be forfeit to the King and bring money to his coffers, and he spent his days riding about the counties tirelessly. When a landowner had made a will and left his estates to another, Nicholas would make enquiries about the character of the heir, reporting to the King so that he would know the manner and type of men who stood to serve in his army should the need arise. Sometimes Nicholas might summon a jury to settle a dispute about inheritance, and everywhere he went he was well respected for his wise and experienced governance.

At home he devoted time to Elizabeth and Edward, ensuring that they received a good upbringing and education. Happily following my wishes, he employed a tutor who was prepared to teach Elizabeth alongside her brother. I had long believed in the importance of learning for girls and was delighted to find our new Queen Katherine a powerful advocate. My husband also agreed whole-heartedly with all my suggestions for improving our manor house at Woodloes. Its age gave it charm but also rendered it draughty and dark, so we embarked on various building works to make it comfortable: larger windows and better fireplaces. I was given free reign to develop the gardens as I pleased and took pleasure in planning and planting a small orchard and nut grove.

In the evenings we would withdraw to the solar or sit companionably by the fire in the hall, as I was used to do with my father. If other men were present, I would listen quietly to their talk, while I embroidered a handkerchief or sewed a sleeve, but when alone we would discuss together the events of the day and the news of the country. One topic that arose soon after the beginning of our married life was young King Henry's determination to stamp his authority on the land. Far from releasing Cousin Bess's father, Richard Empson, he had him charged with treason and beheaded at the Tower.

"Empson's crime was enforcing the old King's laws too strictly," reflected Nicholas. "In essence, he carried out his job too well. He became as unpopular as the taxes he imposed. Young Henry had to make a clean break from the past to ensure his own future."

"But to order someone's death? To end a life? Surely he need not have taken such a final step?" I ventured, thinking of Bess and her grief.

"Sometimes it is the only way there is to go on," he reflected. A rare shade of his past fell between us and I immediately regretted the direction of my questioning, turning the conversation quickly to happier matters.

And there was much to celebrate in our life together. Its highlight was that we were blessed with children. Our marriage proved to be so much more than the relationship of quiet companionship that I had contemplated before our wedding night. After thirty five years a maid, the physical attachment that grew between us, the uncomplicated way in which he would touch me just for the pleasure of it – and my own response of pleasure too – was something quite unexpected. I had never thought to be a mother but our son Ralph, a beautiful strong boy, was born less than a year after our marriage and my little darlings, Anne and Joyce arrived soon after. Most fortunately, I found I gave birth easily and had no cause for secret mumblings or magic. I did not employ Mistress Hyde as my midwife, though Constance still swears by her skill. Instead I looked to Warwick and found a woman well-respected in the town who had brought the sons and daughters of its merchants into this world without resort to superstition, and I put my trust in her.

Nicholas loved his children and delighted to have a growing family. Age did not lessen his enjoyment of their company and although occasionally he sent them away to spare his nerves, I am sure he only behaved as any, much younger, father might do. He had a great sense of fairness and did his best to further the interests of each of his children. He had already settled Baddesley Clinton on Constance and her husband, and now he made conveyances of his manors of Woodloes and Woodcote to provide future income for his sons and security for me in my lifetime. His daughters he knew would make bright marriages, and I believe he began to look out for eligible suitors on the very days that they were born.

Our children were all three christened in St. Nicholas Church, my husband continuing his refusal to receive the sacrament from Robert Banke, and us both finding the quiet humility of the priests and congregation at St. Nicholas better to our taste than the pomp and splendor of Warwick's grander church at the College of St. Mary's. I never understood Nicholas's sudden aversion to Banke, who had served faithfully as his priest for so many years at Baddesley. I never pressed him for the reason but I speculated about it in my own mind, as I do now, kneeling here while Banke intones the closing prayers of this evening's mass. It must have been bound up in some way with my husband's desire to shut out the past. Perhaps he felt it best to break from the priest who had been privy to the most deeply personal moments of his life, heard his confessions, offered comfort in his grief. Whatever was behind the break, as we built our new life together at Woodloes we looked more to Warwick than to Baddesley.

In those happy years, I never raised Katherine's name with Nicholas, though she was often in my thoughts and I spoke of her regularly to Elizabeth and Edward, describing to them the beautiful young lady who was their mother and assuring them of her great affection for them. She had clearly been my husband's one true love: to me he never whispered words of passion but spoke only fondly, calling me 'my own dear girl' or sometimes, 'my darling, Lettice'. Perhaps it is surprising that I was not envious – but I felt only sorrow for her. Perhaps it is strange that I was not more curious about his reasons for not wishing to talk of certain matters – but when I search my soul I find that I respected his desire for silence. Nicholas kept the door on his past with Katherine firmly closed and I was so surprised and pleased to have found this unexpected joy with him that I had no wish to open it.

# IX

The service is ended and the faithful begin to leave the church. Sins forgiven, souls blessed and spirits raised, they trickle away to their homes and families. The priest snuffs out the candles one by one. The stone beneath me is cold as the grave and the gloom becomes darkness. I realize that some hours must have passed since I first sat on the step below the altar to admire the wonderful new window.

What comfort I have gained from my reflections drains away as memories of my husband's end flood in. However we try to prepare ourselves for a loved one's death, however we try to build a strong defence of courage and fortitude, it always cuts us deep. Knowing Nicholas was so much older than me, of course I anticipated that we would not have many years together. I treasured every moment as best I could and even made plans in my own mind about how I would go on without him. He was thoughtful for me too and reassured me that the documents he had drawn up to ensure that his manors and lands would pass to his children, also provided for me to have a good income for my lifetime.

"You will want for nothing, Lettice, when I am gone. I promise you that."

"Hush, husband! Such a time is not worth thinking about. You said as much yourself. Let's just plan what we will do this afternoon. It's a fine one and we could take the children out to the orchard to see how the fruit is ripening."

I tried to follow Nicholas's lead and live only in the present and for the most part I succeeded. It was only in the darkest moments that lines from a poem in my commonplace book stole into my mind,

'Our pleasure here is all vain glory
This false world is but transitory
The flesh is brittle, the Fiend is sly:
*The fear of death disturbs me.*'

Then I would try to persuade myself that my husband was now sixty-seven and his great age must be a sign of God's favour. The bible speaks of three score years and ten, so surely if he lived just three more years, it would show that God had forgiven him for the acts of his youth and if I could convince him of that, he would be able to live his final years untroubled.

But it was not to be. Soon after the apple harvest, he was pierced by a massive pain through the left side of his body that left him gasping and breathless. He had been holding a meeting of his tenants in the hall and Thomas Berkeley was at once beside him. He supported Nicholas and helped him away to a side chamber where I found him slumped in a chair, rubbing his left arm and groaning in discomfort. I opened a window to let in air and then knelt on the floor beside him, wrapping my arms around him and willing him to take my strength.

Thomas and I together struggled to get him to his bed. His dead weight was heavy, for he was a big man still, and muscular. We made him as comfortable as we could and I sent a messenger to ride full speed to Warwick to fetch the physician.

"I'll not recover from this, Lettice," Nicholas whispered as soon as he had regained his breath enough to speak.

"Don't say that! We've sent for the physician and you are a strong man. You know you are."

"No, believe me. This is the end. God has struck me a death blow and now the devil will find me easy pickings."

"Nicholas, don't say such a thing! Just rest quietly now."

Beads of sweat bristled on his forehead and his breath was loud and labored. I put some water to his lips and he drank a little before sinking back on his pillow. But he could not rest.

"The past, every moment of it, must be paid for now. All is laid bare for the fiend to find."

"What are you talking about, Nicholas? You've led a good life, you know you have. Just look around at all you have achieved, the people who have benefitted from your support, the lands that have thrived under your stewardship. Let's have no more talk now, just rest."

"I've dreaded this moment, Lettice. I had hoped it would not come so soon but now it has, it must be faced."

"Are you in much pain?"

He nodded and I saw that he still gripped his left arm and rocked himself a little from side to side. "This is my punishment. It begins now and continues in the fire of Hell where the pain will be worse. I only hope I can bear it."

"Why talk of punishment, Nicholas? You have the Pope's pardon for the sins of your youth, you showed it to me, and the Pope must know God's mind. Pray to God now and you will have nothing to fear."

"Ah, my darling Lettice, my dear girl. How little you know of my sins. The door that I closed on the past after I ... after Katherine. It will be opened now. While I was fit and well, I could keep it barred but now that my flesh begins to weaken, the fiend will find a way to worm through. He will wheedle the wickedness out of me and I must suffer."

I could think of no response, so I mopped the sweat from his brow and held his hand, stroking it to comfort him. Thomas brought me a stool and as I sat beside his bed while he dozed a

123

little, I prayed to Mary, Mother of God, Christ Jesus and all the saints that my husband should recover. I prayed as fervently as I had ever done, urging each word to be heard. I prayed to St. Catherine, my special saint, to look kindly on me, to hear my prayers, that fortune's wheel might turn and restore my husband to good health. As I prayed I was aware of a group of servants huddled just outside the doorway, silent in their concern, and their sympathy gave me strength.

The physician was a capable man, brisk but thorough in his examination. He told me Nicholas's heart was failing. It was beating now but in all probability would give out in a few days. He had seen such cases before: the massive pain was followed by breathlessness and wheezing, a general weakening and then death.

"It is important to make preparations now," he told me. "If Brome has affairs to put in order, now is the time." He patted me on the back, for he was a kind man who still felt sorrow in breaking bad news despite the frequency of doing it. "Be strong for him."

I nodded, "I will try."

Each detail of my husband's dying remains vivid in my mind and for some years afterwards not a day would pass without me reliving part of it, my grief was so consuming.

In body, he rallied a little though he never again left his bed. He insisted on sitting up to greet the many family members and well-wishers who rushed to see him and was able to look out of an open window at the park and the ripening corn in the fields beyond. The pain in his chest eased a little though he was short of breath and tired easily. His mind remained sharp to the end and I am thankful that he never lost his wits as I have seen others do.

His spirit, however, was deeply troubled.

Constance was a great support to me in those few days. She came as soon the news reached her and stayed close by my side. When she heard her father's fear for his soul, she urged him to send for a priest to hear his confession but he would not have it.

"I have no need of confession. I have already repented and received absolution for the sins that can be pardoned. For the rest, God already understands their full extent and can offer no forgiveness. What would be the point of burdening a priest with the knowledge of my wickedness? No, I shall not confess to any priest."

We were both shocked to hear Nicholas describe himself as wicked but he would countenance no persuasion to the contrary.

"By all means, you may send to Warwick for an attorney to write down my will, I am ready to set out the manner I have determined for my burial, but I will not have any priest here. I shall ask the attorney to record that it is my will to be buried standing up, just inside the church door where all who enter will tread on me. It is what I deserve."

"Standing up?" Constance and I both gasped, startled. I had never heard of such a thing. "Nicholas, whatever do you mean?"

"I mean simply that. I have decided to be buried standing up. I will not be laid to rest: for me there will be no rest in death, so why lay me in the earth? I shall have no repose in Heaven; my punishment is to suffer forever the agonies of Hell. I don't know if I shall have the strength to endure these agonies but I will certainly feel better able to face the devil if I am standing up."

Horrified we pleaded with him not to do this. Constance argued that it must be against the teachings of the church, that it was unnatural, that it 'had never been done before and never should be', but he would not change his mind.

"Surely, Nicholas, whatever you have done cannot be so bad that you must suffer in this way," I suggested. "Surely, you cannot know that you will be punished in Hell. People in this world commit terrible crimes, they behave towards others with extreme hatred and cruelty, yet still they confess their sins and, if they are truly sorry, after a time in purgatory they may yet find a place in Heaven. I cannot believe you have done anything to compare with

125

the torture and brutality that some people have inflicted on other poor souls. I know you to be a gentle man."

"Lettice," he said quietly, "I am afraid you don't know me or what I am capable of."

I gave up my protests but Constance persisted as perhaps only a daughter can. "It will disgrace us, Father, it will shame our family. By all means be buried just inside the church, let people tread on you if that is what you want, but not standing up, please. I can't bear to think of it."

Nicholas began to tire of the discussion. A wheezing started deep in his chest, every breath a painful portent of his last.

"Enough, child! To please you, I won't record this in my will but I want you both to know that I desire to be buried standing up and I ask you to respect my wish."

"Rest now, Nicholas, please," I urged him, looking imploringly towards Constance.

"I will make certain it is done. You can be sure of it," she said.

He fell into a doze, leaving Constance and I to our troubled thoughts. I wondered what it was that Nicholas could have done to feel that he deserved such punishment, to be so sure that he would spend eternity in Hell. It pained me to think of it. Certainly, as a young man he had avenged his father's death by killing the murderer, Herthill, and later he had defended the honour of his wife by ending the life of the adulterous priest, but I knew he did not believe he would go to Hell for those sins. He had done penance for them long ago and had confidence in the pardons he received.

"We could find the pardons," I suggested aloud to Constance. "Have them brought from his coffer in the strong room at Baddesley and show them to him. It might help?"

"Yes," she agreed. "Perhaps."

For a moment it crossed my mind that Nicholas might have done some harm to his brother, Thomas: punished him in some way for the smile that was seen on his face in the moment of their father's passing; hastened his death somehow. But of course, in my heart, I knew that the unforgivable sin had something to do with Katherine. Throughout the years of our marriage, I had allowed Nicholas to remain silent about his time with her but now the past he would never speak of demanded to be heard.

"Did he mistreat Katherine?" I asked Constance. "Did he harm her in some way? I cannot think him capable but he must have done something to damn himself so utterly."

"No, I've asked myself that and I'm sure there was nothing. He loved Katherine completely. I saw them together often and there was never any sign. She was his joy!" She looked at me rather hesitantly.

"Don't fear offending me. I have always known she was the love of his life. The only mystery was that he never talked about her. I would have been happy to hear of their time together. I was fond of her too."

We sat on in silent contemplation until the attorney arrived and Nicholas was roused to dictate his will.

"Father, you may feel there is no hope for your soul but I believe in a merciful God. If you are truly repentant and confess your sins, he will forgive you. I honestly believe it. Please make provision in your will for masses to be sung for your soul. Don't give up all hope," Constance begged him.

"For you, my child, I will enlist the prayers of all I can, though my hope of salvation was lost long ago."

He was confident and lucid as he set out the terms of his will,

"In God's name Amen: the third day of October in the year of our Lord God one thousand five hundred and sixteen. I, Nicholas Brome of Woodloes, being of sound mind and good memory, thanks be to Almighty God, do make and ordain this my testament and last will in the following manner: First I bequeath my soul unto Almighty God, my Creator and Saviour, to our Lady, Saint Mary, and to all the saints, and my body to be buried within the church door of the parish church of St. James in Baddesley, there as people may tread upon me when they come into the church."

Nicholas paused and smiled at me with his warm brown eyes before moving swiftly on, "I will that there be ordained and laid upon my grave a flat stone of marble with a brass image and an inscription recording the day and year of my decease and my coat of arms, with the intention that hereafter I might be better remembered and prayed for."

Constance nodded her encouragement and he went on to bequeath money to the priests, friars and clerks who would say mass or sing dirges at his funeral and one penny to each poor man who would come to his burying and pray for him. He willed that a mass should be said for his soul every year for the next ten years in the church at Baddesley and that masses should be said for his soul and dirges sung in all the holy places where he was a brother: Corpus Christi and the Convent of the Grey Friars in Coventry; the Guild Chapel and the Priory of Black Friars in Warwick; the Convent of St. Mary's in Worcester, where his first wife, Elizabeth, came from; the Convent at Wroxall, where his sister, Jocosa Joyce was Prioress, and the Guild Chapel in Knowle, where his dead babies were commemorated. As he listed these places that had meant so much to him and where he would be fondly remembered, tears came to my eyes and I felt bewilderment that his outlook should be so bleak. Surely, with all these people praying for him, there was some hope for his soul?

He ended by setting out the provisions he had made already for his children: Constance and Edward Ferrers were to have Baddesley Clinton, his son Edward would have the manors of Woodloes, Overwoodcote and Netherwoodcote when he came of age, and Ralph would have lands that Nicholas had recently purchased in Shirley specifically to ensure that his youngest son, our son, would be well provided for. The income generated from these lands and manors before the boys came of age would be used to support me and to provide dowries for Elizabeth, Anne and Joyce. He had thought everything through so carefully and I loved him for it. As executors, he appointed Constance and a very eminent local landowner, Sir Edward Greville. Edward Ferrers was named as overseer. It was all done correctly and with proper dignity.

Would this man suffer in Hell? I could not believe it and for a moment I felt a swell of anger towards Nicholas for putting me through this unnecessary pain. My emotions were on the wheel, for the next moment I was suppressing sobs of sorrow as he signed the will in his bold, round hand and I felt he was signing his life away and it was all too soon.

His last days passed quietly. Constance and I took turns to sit beside him. It was hard to see his body giving up its strength. Frailty was something he had never experienced before and he took it as a sign that God was deserting him.

"And it is right that God should leave me now. There were days when I felt close to Him. We were happy together, weren't we, Lettice?"

"We were, husband – We are."

"But sometimes the trials He sets us are too cruel, unjust even. You see, my dear, I challenge Him even now: my fate is sealed."

"You have a strong sense of justice and you've always acted on it. That can't be a sin before God. But, Nicholas, I am no theologian. Please, make your confession to a priest. Whatever it is that you have done, confess it, be penitent, ask God's forgiveness. It is not too late."

"I cannot Lettice, for I am not sorry. I don't regret what I did, I have no remorse and would act in the same way again, if the situation arose."

"Please, Nicholas. Let me send for a priest."

"Believe me, my dear, if I could please you and Constance by making a confession, I would do so. To upset you is the last thing I wish, but it can't be done. I cannot ask to be forgiven for something for which I am not sorry. God is no fool to be duped with insincerity."

I saw there would be no persuading him and my heart was heavy. I couldn't begin to imagine him experiencing the torments of Hell, but I knew that he was suffering now.

"You should not take the knowledge of your sin to your grave alone but share it with someone, please, I beg you. To share it will make your burden lighter. Please, if you will not confess to a priest, then confess to me."

Nicholas let out a deep sigh as he pondered this and the sigh ended with a wheeze that he could not clear by coughing.

"Oh Nicholas, husband, please confide in me. Tell me what it is that you have done, so you can go quietly to your grave."

Finding his breath he murmured, "I killed her, Lettice."

"Who? Katherine?" I asked doubtfully. "No husband, you did not kill her. She died in childbirth, remember? I was there. It was a terrible time but there was nothing anyone could have done to save her."

"I killed her. I wish that it was otherwise, but it is true."

"Nicholas, it was not your fault that she died. She was young, yes, but she had borne other children. There was no reason to suppose…"

"She was in agony – you know, you saw how she suffered." He gathered his strength. "The midwife told me there was no hope for her and nothing she could do to end her pain. I asked to be alone with her and took her in my arms. She was burning, shaking and sweating. I strained to make out her mumbling but it made no sense. As I lay her down gently, I told her of my love and placed a soft pillow over her face. I held it there until her rasping breath was quiet and her misery was over. It only took a moment. So, you see it is true. I killed her."

I closed my eyes and sat in silence letting this truth sink in. I didn't know how to respond, I had no response. All I could do was let words come to me and hope that later I would think I had said the right thing.

"It was an act of kindness, Nicholas. Anyone would see it so."

"Not God."

"God knows you acted to end her suffering. He is a merciful God."

We fell quiet again.

"You deserve a place in Heaven, Nicholas, you really do. I sincerely believe that and pray that it will be so."

"You won't tell anyone? Not Constance?"

"No, I won't tell a soul," I took his hand and squeezed it firmly. "But Nicholas, I think, when you are ready, when you feel the time is right, you should make your last confession to a priest. You need not be specific but make what peace with God you can. It will help us all."

He pressed my hand in reply and smiled into my eyes. "Lettice, you are right and you are the best of women. I'll do it."

And so, the following day as he became weaker and knew the time of his death was near, Nicholas asked me to send for his family and for a priest to hear his last confession, "Not Banke."

"No, don't fret, I'll not summon Reverend Banke."

It is said that there is an art to dying. Books have been written on the subject and I wanted to make everything right for him. With the help of our servants, I prepared his room, hanging a crucifix above his bed and placing on the table beside him a beautifully illuminated bible and the brass statue of his sister Jocosa Joyce, now prioress of Wroxall, that his mother had treasured. I sent for a barber to trim his hair and beard and a manservant to wash him and dress him in his richest clothes. It pleased Nicholas to look his best, though it broke my heart to see him a pale shadow of the fine man he was. His family gathered around the bed:

Constance and Edward with their children; Dorothy; Elizabeth and Edward, then eleven and nine years old; and my little ones, Ralph, Anne and Joyce, with their nursemaid. In the passageway outside his room and in the hall below, his household and well-wishers congregated.

The priest, when he arrived, looked around and saw that all was well arranged. He spoke to us of death as something to be welcomed and not to be afraid of and urged Nicholas to avoid the temptations that can beset a dying man: the loss of faith, the descent into despair. We were all told to prepare for our own death and to be ever ready to meet our God. The atmosphere could not have been more sombre and even the children were chilled to silence. Hardly able to speak, Nicholas whispered his confession to the priest and was given absolution. Three silver boxes hung from the priest's belt and from two of them he now took a wafer of bread and a phial of wine for the viaticum, the preparation for the journey into death. It was hard to rouse Nicholas to swallow the bread, and the wine just touched his lips, but the last rites were administered in the proper way. The third box held holy oil to anoint the dying. The priest dipped his middle finger in the oil and, uttering the words of blessing, bent over Nicholas and made the sign of the cross upon his forehead. As he did so, I saw him gently close my husband's eyes.

Prayers were now said for Nicholas, the first of many that would be offered up in the years to come: prayers in thanks for his long and fruitful life, prayers to ease the passage of his soul through purgatory and into Heaven. We all joined sincerely in saying each 'Amen' but he was not there to hear us. Tears welled in my eyes. To the world it would seem that he had died a good death, only he and I knew the truth, but whether his death was good or bad, it made no matter. He was gone.

I realize that here in the church the priest is moving around extinguishing the candles and only two remain. I have to leave, so

I stand up, brushing out the creases from my gown and replacing the hair that has strayed from beneath my cap.

I remember the pain of those first years after his death, when it seemed that the purpose had gone from my life and his physical presence, which I had so loved, was replaced not by emptiness but by a terrible confusion, a tangle of thoughts and feelings that first demanded to be unpicked, then caught me in their web. However much I tried to distract myself with the practicalities of daily life – and there was much to do – my mind was always full of the most vivid images of my husband: pressing a pillow over Katherine's face; being tormented by unspeakable tortures in Hell; lying on his deathbed and begging me to tell no-one; bending to kiss my hand in the stable yard the day we met. Dread of his agony overwhelmed me. Now, in my stronger moments, I doubt that he actually killed Katherine and cling to the hope that in his state of shock at losing her, he imagined it all, or I reassure myself that if he did indeed kill her, God would judge it to be an act of mercy. I reason this and yet my dread remains.

"I don't mean to hasten the end of your prayers, Mistress Brome," says the priest as he picks up the final candle and comes towards me. "You are welcome to remain if you wish. I can leave this light for you."

I see the priest is Robert Banke. I knew all through the service that it was him, of course, still faithfully serving the family and parish at Baddesley after all these years. I just didn't notice until now. I wonder why Nicholas took against him so.

"Thank you, that's kind. I think I may stay a while."

Banke had prayed with Nicholas immediately after Katherine died. Was it possible that Nicholas might have told him the terrible thing he had done? That might explain the rift between them. And if Banke had been privy to the state of my husband's soul, maybe he could tell me something that would bring me some comfort.

"In fact, perhaps you would have a few minutes to sit with me?" I suggest. "Now I think about it, there is something I'd like to ask you."

"Ah, so the moment has come." He sits down, placing the candle on the pew beside him. "I anticipated that one day you'd wish to speak with me".

I sit with the light between us and wonder where to begin. "My husband told me something before he died, something about Katherine's death – Katherine, his second wife."

"Ah, yes."

"You were at the house, I know. You saw him afterwards, after she was gone. Did he say anything surprising to you?"

"My dear, let's be open with each other. Let's not think ourselves to be breaking a confidence if we speak frankly now. I believe we are already party to a secret that troubles both our souls. Perhaps in sharing our concerns we might find peace."

I feel a huge weight fall from my shoulders. So, he knows. "Just as my husband was dying, he confided in me that he had ended Katherine's misery, he'd hastened her death by suffocating her with a pillow."

"Yes, he confessed as much to me. He was calm but deeply troubled. It seemed his heart was broken."

"So he made a confession to you and you absolved him," I say with relief.

"No, my dear. I wish it had been so. But no, I could not give him absolution, for he was not sorry for what he had done. He was not penitent. I begged him to show some remorse for his sin and to ask God for forgiveness, but he would not."

"I believe he felt it was right to end her pain," I reflect. "He was always straightforward and acted in the way he saw to be most honorable. Perhaps, for him, to let her suffer would have been the sin." I am thinking aloud. "Was this the cause of the break between you?"

"I was the only person who knew what he had done," says Banke. "I think by distancing himself from me, he was able to separate himself from the act. He knew he would be damned but he chose to take his pleasure while he could and live his final years in happiness."

"Do you believe him damned? He was such a good man, a gentle man."

"Life is sacred, Mistress Brome. God gives us life and it is not ours to take. Murder, as you know, is a mortal sin."

"Then you do believe he is in Hell? I have been wracked with pain and doubt. I cannot bear to imagine his suffering."

"Perhaps the question is not so much what I believe," suggests Banke, "as what our reason tells us. God gave us life and He also gave us reason to make sense of it. What does your reason tell you? Did Nicholas sin in ending Katherine's life?"

"I have tried to convince myself that he did not," I say. "I told him it was an act of kindness – and it was, wasn't it? Katherine was in terrible pain. She was delirious. I saw her myself. Ending her suffering was like killing a rabbit caught in a trap, a merciful deed. The church may argue that killing is wrong but instinctively we know we are right to put the rabbit out of its misery. It wasn't a mortal sin, surely?"

"There are certainly some who argue that alleviating suffering near death should not be viewed as murder. The great thinker, Thomas More, included such an idea when he wrote of an imaginary land called 'Utopia' that was free of religious doctrine and built entirely on reason. There it was no sin to aid someone in willingly letting go of their life if they were in agony and had no hope of recovery."

"Perhaps that is how God sees it," I urge. "I know Nicholas acted out of compassion not cruelty."

"Ah, compassion. Some will say they act out of compassion to end another's suffering when in truth it is their own suffering they wish to stop. They cannot bear to see the one they love in pain or torment. It hurts them too much. They cannot endure it themselves. I think in settling Nicholas's case, we must determine his intention."

I consider this. It seems to touch on the heart of the matter.

"My husband was a strong man, well able to endure his own suffering. He had no intention of benefiting from her death – Katherine was everything to him and her death brought him more pain, not less. No, his thought was all for Katherine. His intention was only to spare her agony. His was not a selfish act."

"Then I think we may reason that he acted out of pure compassion?"

"He knew she was near death," I remind him. "We all knew that; there was no other way for her. Perhaps her soul departed even before he extinguished her last breath; perhaps God had already taken back her life."

I remember Nicholas lying on his deathbed, with all of us around him, praying for him, and he already gone.

"Then we could see his act as no more a crime than the closing of a dead one's eyes?" says Banke.

This seems to be an ending. I stand and thank the priest for his time. I touch his arm and feel through his vestments that he is thin now and old.

"Our talk has been comforting," I assure him.

He sits on in the dying light of the candle, perhaps less certain.

I cross the silent church and, as I open the heavy door, I pause for a moment on my husband's grave. He is not there. Stepping outside into a starry night, I turn and hurry along the path, through the avenue of sturdy oaks he planted, towards the welcoming lights of the manor house and the warmth of our waiting family.

# Author's Note

The flat stone of marble and brass image of Nicholas Brome have long since been removed from the church at Baddesley Clinton in Warwickshire, England. Perhaps the Victorians felt he did not deserve such commemoration. But from the moment I pulled aside the doormat to reveal the simple stone that now marks his grave, I knew his story had to be told.

Researching the extraordinary history of Nicholas Brome took me deep into the archives of the Warwickshire County Record Office and the Shakespeare Birthplace Trust; to the historical writings of Edmond Hawes, Sir William Dugdale and Rev. Henry Norris; and to modern works such as 'Locality and polity: A study of Warwickshire landed society, 1401-1499' by Christine Carpenter and 'The Masculine Self in Late Medieval England' by Derek G. Neal; but it left many gaps that could only be filled by my imagination and this is a work of fiction. Lettice (or Letitia) Catesby became Nicholas Brome's third wife, bore him three children and finally buried him, yet she is almost absent from the historical record. This absence inspired me to create a voice for her and it was then a pleasure to explore her perspective on her husband's eventful life as she sought salvation for his soul.

# Acknowledgements

In unearthing this story and writing my first novel, I had huge support from my husband, Paul Elliott, who probably felt on more than one occasion that he would prefer Nicholas Brome to lie quietly in his grave, yet never failed to encourage me. Paul has my sincere thanks and love. My daughters, Hannah and Francesca, have been an inspiration: from their excitement as children when visiting the National Trust property of Baddesley Clinton to their faith in my ability to do justice to the story of Nicholas Brome. I thank them both. I am also very grateful to the friends who read my first draft and gave me such helpful feedback: Elizabeth Dean, whose enthusiasm and assistance with my research was invaluable, Susan Lawrence and Tamara Hoogerdyk.

My last word goes to the beautiful English county of Warwickshire. Its ancient towns and footpaths, manor houses and meadows inspired this tale.

# About the Author

Anne Elliott now lives in Peterborough, Ontario but her roots are in the stories and history of the United Kingdom. Born in Hampshire, she lived and worked in Wales and Wiltshire before settling for sixteen years in Kenilworth, Warwickshire – the heart of England – with her husband and two daughters. Since the family's move to Canada in 2007, she has had the opportunity for historical research and writing. She enjoys exploring the history and culture of her new country and supporting other immigrants and refugees.